The Mountain Monk and Shadow Rider

Book Three of 'The Ultimate Link' Series

LIZZIE COLLINS

"Striding towards us, it seemed to me in slow-motion, was the austere, authoritative person of my father.

Wow! In his own environment he was a king. People actually moved aside to let him pass.

I looked at him, mouth open, impressed beyond measure. Occasionally a runner would approach him with a paper to read, occasionally an autograph to sign but he brushed them away like flies. His eyes were fixed on mine and he was not to be distracted."

Anna Christina Maxwell Robson

ISBN: 9798835764167

Acknowledgement

A huge thank you to the multitude of writers and friends who have mostly innocently, provided the background to this story.

The Internet has given a latitude to research Jane Austen could never have imagined so – thank you too Messrs. Page and Brin for your contribution.

Final page quotation:

Lines from 'The End' from the 'Abbey Road' album credited to Paul McCartney

Prologue

Christie

So Pa finally heard me play piano and I must say I was very gratified by his reaction, although I could have done without the major trauma he put me through at the beginning.

Playing for him the very first time when he sang the blues - was an experience beyond my wildest dreams. So not only was he my Pa but he'd become my hero too.

I'd played the odd Uni gig from time to time but as the standard of my co-bandmembers was pretty iffy at best, I hadn't had much to compare myself to, except my Guardian Bobby – who turned out to be my uncle – who was a clever all-rounder.

It had been a very tangled web. But everything should be straight forward from now on.

For a start, I now knew who my birth parents were, who my Guardians and step-mother were, where I'd been born, who my adopted parents were – God bless 'em – and I owned the most fabulous diamond engagement ring and the guy who went with it. Plain sailing.

I'd be Mrs. Simeon Maxwell next Spring, hopefully in a snowstorm of apple blossom and lace, and babies one, two and three before I was twenty five. Two girls and a boy I'd thought.

There might be a bit of a squabble as to who should lead me down the aisle – Connie and I would enjoy watching Pa and Dad duke it out.

The one cloud on my horizon was that Pa had point-blank refused to budge over helping me with my ambition to follow in his footsteps and become a major musician.

He said I'd have to decide between babies and the piano and I was choosing the babies.

1

I repeatedly shed tears when I thought about my darling Grace and the desperately sad way she'd left us. I was so disappointed Pa never got to meet her. If anyone could have sorted him out it would have been Grace. After she caught him drunk or out of it on cocaine, her reaction would have been along the lines of:

"Oh, for the love of God, pull yourself together, You're out of short pants – stop behaving like a goddam brat."

Except her language would probably have been more colorful.

Connie and I, Simm, Giulia and my Guardians – all but Sunny – had had our lives indisputably enriched by her part in them.

Simm and I would miss our adored grandmother until the day we died.

Chapter One

Windfall

Christie

All the way back to Champaign the morning after the second performance, Simm and I sang. We massacred the California Crystal Band harmonies and laughed hysterically at each other's shortcomings.

No scrunchy on earth would have held my streaming hair so eventually I gave up and contented myself with the occasional spitting out of wisps caught in my mouth.

The last words Simm said to me before we walked through the door were:

"Tell your Mom and Dad about seeing your Pa on stage but don't mention what the two of you discovered when you played together. That kind of love would hurt them."

That could be put on a back burner for an hour or two since Dad was at work and Mom was out at her friend Eileen's. Wonderful!

I took the ring out of my purse and put it back on, twisting my hand this way and that to catch the light. I kissed my man with passion then nearly fell up the stairs trying to climb them without taking my eyes off the diamonds.

There'd be no separate rooms after today and I shifted all his belongings into mine before we set to sealing our engagement…. again.

"I could get used to this," I gasped against his lips.

Once the initial intensity had subsided, we spent a few days trying to convince my Mom and Dad they hadn't been written out of my life, although I had to admit, lately, they pretty much had.

Simm invited them to San Clemente, but first he'd to go to Los Angeles to see his Dad and talk to him about Grace's Will, which he was looking forward to like toothache. But he'd be back in San Clemente within a few days. Sooner, if humanly possible.

He begged me to go with him. Being the daughter of Oliver's arch-enemy Gil Robson, I didn't think that would be a good move, but I agreed to go and stay with Connie in Santa Monica to be at hand should he need me.

It's a long way from Illinois to California. By the time the plane touched down, Simm was all for calling Mom and Dad and telling them he loved Champaign so much he was coming right back. I truly think, left to himself, he would have done just that. Unfortunately for him, he wasn't.

We parted ways at the airport and took cabs, he to Bel Air and I to Santa Monica. He held on for grim death as he kissed me goodbye.

"Go...away! The sooner you get there the sooner you can leave."

His iron grip loosened, and he got in the cab as if he was mounting a tumbril. I rolled my eyes and got in the next car in line. But a small part of me did guiltily think 'rather him than me'.

Connie was all hugs and kisses. She'd just got back from a shopping expedition and there were packages scattered all over the sofa and some, larger, propped against its arm.

After greeting me, she went back to sorting them, muttering to herself as she did so:

"Ah! This one's for you!"

She handed over a small soft parcel wrapped in pink paper. I loved surprises.

Inside, wrapped in silver tissue was a cream bolero cardigan with abalone buttons of the palest violet. It was as delicate as swansdown.

"How kind of you – I love it. Thank you so much."

I tried it on and pirouetted in front of the mirror.

"It's perfect!" And it truly was.

When Simm reappeared the following day, he'd two deep scratches on the left side of his face. They were red and angry-looking. Connie took one look and her face contorted in fury.

"Don't tell me…Deborah! And don't you dare look like that at me,"

He'd immediately taken on his placatory manner but it clearly didn't wash with Connie.

"She was in the room with Dad and me when I was explaining the bequest and went at me like a hellcat. I can't think what I did to upset her."

"Sounds like fifty million dollars and a car sort of upset to me," I said wryly.

"Guess you're right. She was mad enough for both of them. Dad went as white as a sheet but I could see the cogs already turning as to how he could wriggle his way through this and get the Will declared void."

I laughed.

"Well, I wish him luck with that. Grace was nothing if not thorough."

But it worried me just the same.

We stopped overnight although Connie pressed us to stay longer. I explained about my parents and she nodded her agreement.

"You should go, but don't forget your Momma Connie will be waiting,"

I laughed at her choice of words.

"Well, I am. Aren't I? It's not fair that you call Julius and Cathy Mom and Dad and have even taken to calling Gil, Pa. What about me?" she said defensively.

"Yep," I replied. "Mom and Dad, Pa and Ma sound great."

"Don't you dare call me that. That's what Jacob used to call me when he was little. He got it from the TV and I used to get really cross with him."

"Connie it is then," I grinned.

She hugged Simm and me and kissed our cheeks. I could tell she loved him deeply and it was returned.

We drove down to San Clemente stopping at a roadhouse for a bite to eat. As we drove past Ed's mansion, we saw a realtor's sign advertising its sale so we turned in out of curiosity.

Maurice was still there, still as dour.

He told us his employment was terminating at the end of that month. He hadn't found anything else locally so it looked as if his kids would be changing schools. That was one of those very rare times I saw him express emotion. Momentarily, he looked forlorn. Simm was compassionate as always.

"Would you consider working for me? It'll mean relocating your children's school though. San Clemente is too far away for them to travel."

"Word please, my love." We walked out of earshot.

"For chrissake, Simm. You don't own Ginsling House. Grace alone knows who does but it certainly isn't us."

He started laughing at my expression and walked back to Maurice, still chortling.

Maurice looked almost excited. Well, for him anyway.

"Are you serious, Mr....er?"

"Simeon Maxwell – but call me Simm. If you must add Mr. make it Simeon. Mr. Simm sounds like a character in a kid's book. And yes, I am serious."

So Mr. Maxwell it was from then on.

"There's a staff cottage out back of the main house. It's not huge – three bedrooms. You can move in any time you like but sooner rather than later, always assuming we can agree terms,"

"My deepest thanks," said Maurice, looking determined. "I'll start the move next week if that will be convenient."

"Simm!" I exclaimed, in a stage whisper. "You can't do that with someone else's property."

He ignored me and swinging the car keys round his finger walked off down the drive to the car.

It was about another hour's journey to Ginsling House. In all that time, all he did was grin like an idiot and sing loudly to the radio. To me he said not one word.

Once he'd parked, he fairly skipped up the drive to the door.

Over breakfast the following morning he told me he was going to call his legal firm about a contract of employment for Maurice. I thought that wise because he didn't know him and slapping me around was hardly a recommendation.

He walked to the car in the autumn sunshine and smiled and waved as he drove away.

I rang the staff and asked them to come in as soon as they could.

In the meantime, I cleared the dirty china from the table on the terrace, put it in the dishwasher then did a general tidy round.

Simm's only real fault was he was appallingly untidy. When we'd arrived the day before, he'd dropped his bag on the floor in the hall and thrown his jacket over the tapestry chair. His briefcase had flipped open as it landed with force and some of the contents had scattered across the floor.

I put everything in its proper place, pushed the contents back into the briefcase and took it to the small room Simm was in the process of transforming into an office. Why was a complete mystery.

There were floor to ceiling windows on one wall which overlooked Maurice's new home. The bookshelves were in place but his books, with a few exceptions, were still packed in boxes. His desk had been moved from his father's house but had an old kitchen chair as a temporary seat.

Several sheets of paper were in a neat pile on the desk, and as I placed the briefcase beside them, I couldn't resist a quick glance. I have many failings but the worst was and always had been, curiosity.

On top of the pile was a manilla envelope with my name written in Grace's hand. I picked it up. It wasn't sealed and anyway anything with my name on it must be my business I argued, even if I'd come across it by accident. I tried to walk away but the envelope pulled me back like a magnet.

The house was empty. No-one need ever know.

I unfolded the contents of the envelope and spread them out on the desk. They were dated January eighteen years previously. I realized with a jolt they were the original deeds to this very house made out in Grace's name, and they bore her bold

8

signature.

I looked furtively over my shoulder. Silence.

A second sheet was appended. My mouth fell open as I read:

"The afore-mentioned property with all its contents is held in trust by me, Grace Maxwell, for my adopted granddaughter Anna Christina Heywood aka Robson. Full ownership is to be transferred to her on the occasion of her marriage, twenty-first birthday or my death, whichever occurs first"

Whhaaattt!

A splutter from behind me quickly turned into laughter.

"I knew you'd never resist it," he gasped. "I knew once you saw your name you just would never be able to leave it be.."

He did a gleeful little jig.

"This was a set up? The whole god-damned thing was a set up. You bastard!"

He danced and laughed harder. I picked up the closest item to hand, his briefcase, and hit him with it.

Somehow we ended up on the floor, all legal matters forgotten.

Chapter Two

Reappraisal and New Beginning

Gil

There is a Spirit, a light in the dark, which controls our lives with or without our consent.

Always, I had tried to find my way through the trials of this world. Sometimes I thought I understood only to find the truth had eluded and made a fool of me.

In my younger days I examined every avenue, experimented to the point of harm to my body and soul. I stood on the very brink of existence and looked down the unfathomable chasm which was my life. It was deserted and lonely.

My poor adored brother fared even worse. He is lost for good, never to be held in my arms again. He was my closest friend, a dear soul to the end, but chained to a sadness which destroyed him.

There was never a point where I ever felt I had control. I would think I did, then be buffeted sideways into another path by circumstance. Always thrown this way and that, bashed and thumped from side to side.

Yet no-one ever saw this in me. I was always the one with the strength to carry others, to sort problems, to mend fences. Except I wasn't.

I lost the love of my life to matters outside my control. I will worship her until I draw my last breath but she is as dead to me as the grave.

Her successor is a dear soul, sweet and kind. She loves me with all her being, but she is an innocent, a child. The pain I cause her is a dagger in my heart.

My faith – and even that was tarnished - was all that remained to me, kept me alive and whole.

The candle-flame of my life was my music. When I sang a perfect soaring note my soul went with it, lifting me to another plane. Every song held at least one such note.

One song alone was composed of light. My friends in the audience understood this and felt its power. The people in my personal life had long ago stopped seeing me.

And then, at my lowest ebb – when all I wanted was to join Jamie in blessed peace - came my savior, my Christie. Born of stupidity and selfishness she became my shining light.

I desperately needed her to understand.

So, I prodded and searched trying one last time for the truth which had always eluded me.

It came to me loud, strong and pure on a deserted stage in Chicago. And I wasn't even trying.

I stared moodily out of the window of our chartered jet at the handful of glittering lights scattered haphazardly on the blackness far below. New York. Not our destination. I couldn't remember where that was. They all seemed the same: download equipment and us, play, pack up equipment, sleep and on to the next place. For over twenty years the same songs until I felt flattened by the boredom of it all. I arranged and rearranged the music until my imagination ran out.

I had found her, my daughter, and had to leave her without knowing her. It was unbearable.

My notebook with scribbled details of the dates yet to play, told of another week of commitments. Then I'd drop everything and fly to Los Angeles. I wouldn't sleep - I'd drive to San Clemente immediately.

I had to be sure what I'd seen and heard in Chicago was no figment of my imagination.

Then I'd ring Giulia in Denver and take Christie and Simm to our mountain hide-away. There were few people I could share its crystal silence with. I'd have to see if they fit.

The days until the tour finished ran into each other. I was short tempered where before I had been patient. Bobby kept getting me coffee and burgers and looking worried. It did nothing to stop my irritation.

Finally.... finally, I arrived at Christie's front door in San Clemente. She made me sleep.

The following morning came as something of a shock. Rather than being alone with Christie and Simm, Julius and Catherine had come to spend a few days with them.

"Mom, Dad – this is Gil Robson," said Christie as she made room for me at the terrace table.

What should I say? I was at a loss. Simm was my man instantly when he said:

"He's a fairly good singer and plays a bit of guitar. Apart from that, he's a regular guy."

Christie frowned at him.

"They already know that, idiot! Say something useful."

"Okay. Gil, this is Cathy and Julius Heywood, Christie's parents."

Christie looked heavenward, and I could see Simm was going to pay for that remark. That made me chuckle - they clearly had fun together.

I liked Julius. I felt I understood him. He'd a permanently

worried expression and a habit of deferring to other opinions. He held out his hand which I shook.

"I'm glad to know you, Gil. Christie has spoken of no-one else since she first met you," he shrugged ruefully. "I would be jealous if her life hadn't been given to us for the eighteen years you missed."

That stung. I deserved it.

"Here, Pa" said Christie and I saw Cathy wince.

My little girl passed me a coffee too hot to drink and some toast which I almost choked on.

"I didn't know you'd be here," I said to Cathy. "I've just gotten back off tour and came straight here. Christie knew I was coming but had no idea when. I'm sorry to interrupt your time together. I have some business I can attend to in LA. I can come back later."

"The hell you will!" said Simm. "We're all big enough to deal with this."

He looked round the table, pointedly daring anyone to disagree.

"You'll embarrass everyone, Sim. Can it."

"What?" he said in mock-bewilderment. "I was trying for the opposite."

"Failed dismally there, Simm." I said and couldn't suppress a grin.

I was pleased I stayed. Christie's adopted parents were good people. Not exciting to a person of her temperament, but they'd kept her safe and sound for so many years. I was surprised that I felt relieved rather than resentful.

I wasn't exactly a genius around children although I had tried with Jamie's for a while after he died. In retrospect I realized that was more for him than them. My own two boys, Christie's stepbrothers, were a mystery however. I wondered how they'd take my friendship with their sister. Probably by now, the whole subject would have bored them.

I knew Christie's adult life belonged to me. So did Julius and Cathy and they were resigned. I think they must always have known how things would be. They would not be cut out of her life though – I would make sure of that.

My friendship with my daughter seemed to have been tacitly accepted by all, even Connie which was a relief.

I'd forgotten so quickly the very thing which had shocked me when I first saw Christie. She was in no way a clone of Connie. She was almost her double in appearance, but her character was so different. It was as if she and Simm were as Connie and I should have been.

Julius and Cathy left after a few days. He'd to return to work. The handshake, I'm sure for both of us, was genuine but tinged with relief. Cathy smiled her goodbye but stood back behind her husband to avoid further contact.

I stayed on an extra couple of days which also proved interesting.

In conversation with Simm, I learned Grace had left me a few thousand dollars "for services rendered." This spoke volumes for the character of this old lady and I was sorry I had never known her.

I told Christie, if Probate went through okay, she should take my portion and donate it to a charity of her choice. I didn't know the lady, and after all the services rendered had not been unpleasant, but I kept that thought to myself.

Next day I'd to return to LA for more studio work.

Before I left, I stood them dinner at a good restaurant.

When the subject of conversation came round to Christie's keyboard skills, as it must of course, it was Simm who suggested I might give her a try away from an audience in the studio. Only Bobby would know who she was, and it would mean so much to her.

Thankfully, he'd been tactful enough to wait until she'd visited the restroom. I stopped and thought about it for a few minutes but then I could see her coming back, so I signaled Simm to change the subject.

"Speak later," I whispered across the table.

"What have you two got you heads together about?" said my observant daughter.

Simm was a quick thinker.

"Oh nothing. Just telling him about Maurice. He thinks it's a good idea too."

I tried to look as if I had a clue what he was talking about. It must have been successful because she let the matter drop.

The opportunity to speak to Simm didn't arise again before I left the following day. I was so loath to leave, I said my goodbyes on the terrace. This time I hugged them both and said looking pointedly at Simm, I'd call in the next few days.

Christie gave me a kiss on the cheek which melted my heart. My knee-jerk reaction was to back away in fear. She noticed and kissed me again, squeezing my hand. I left hurriedly, only breathing properly once I'd hit the freeway.

Chapter Three

An Unexpected Gift from Pa and Simm

Christie

Simm seemed to be a bit on edge once Pa had gone. Perhaps it was understandable – I felt the same way. He'd so quickly become a fixture in my life. The bond, which had been so instantaneous, had left me floundering. I really did understand his consternation when I kissed him goodbye.

He'd filled a gap in Simm's life too.

Connie wasn't the most maternal of women, but he'd taken to her straight away. From what Connie said, Oliver and Deborah presented a united front and Simm was often excluded. So, as Pa was a new fixture in my life, perhaps Simm saw him in the same light. I could see they were developing a firm friendship.

A couple of days passed. Then one morning, Simm told me to pack a bag and get in the car. I was getting used to his ways by now and pictured a beach on Hawaii or skiing in the Rockies – not that I could ski. It might be fun to learn though.

He remained tight-lipped, literally. Every time I spoke, he pressed his finger to his lips and made shushing noises.

As we neared LA we turned away from the coast along the San Gabriel freeway. So… we weren't taking a plane anywhere. Where could we drive from east LA? We bypassed the downtown area heading for Hollywood. No. Why the hell would he take me there? No way! But before we got there, he turned west down Santa Monica Boulevard, bypassing the haunt of endless tourists and pulling into the parking lot of a large, non-descript red brick building.

"We're here!" said Simm.

"Here where?" I asked confused. He marched towards the glass door.

"Simm! This is no longer funny. Just where in the hell are we?"

He threw open the door and pointed to the wall behind the reception desk, where in bold letters were the words 'Westlake Recording Studios."

I was so intent of getting out of my beloved fiancé where we were, that despite the noise I had failed to notice the activity. Dozens of people dashing back and forth in organized chaos. It was as busy as a beehive.

There were doors with studio numbers on them, some flung wide and displaying huge consoles and microphones of assorted designs, some with stands and coils of wire tucked away neatly.

"What the hell are we doing here?" I yelled over the cacophony of shouts, the occasional shriek of feedback and muted tuning-up.

Then all was revealed.

Striding towards us, it seemed to me in slow-motion, was the austere, authoritative person of my Pa.

Wow! In his own environment he was a king. People actually moved aside to let him pass.

I looked at him, mouth open, impressed beyond measure. Occasionally a runner would approach him with a paper to read, occasionally an autograph to sign but he brushed them away like flies. His eyes were fixed on mine and he was not to be distracted.

He stood in front of me. My mouth still agape, he picked me up in his habitual bearhug and jiggled me around until one of my earrings dropped out. All the hype disappeared and there stood my Pa, looking like a schoolboy playing hooky.

Then, once more, he was serious.

"You are not to mention to anyone here who you are. I've told Bobby he's fired if he lets slip."

"I think you're needed back at work," I grinned, looking pointedly behind him.

He turned and saw a line of musicians, all smirking. They clearly thought I was some kind of loose woman.

"Back to work. Steve, I want tacks on those hammers. Don, we'll try that again with different percussion - softer - xylophone with dampened mallets. Todd – you're the engineer, so back in the box - I'll be there when I've finished up here."

They gradually melted away before he found them extra work.

He turned his back on them and gave me a wink - I'd never take him seriously again.

Simm had wandered off and was looking out of the glass doors. He was lousy at keeping a straight face, so he'd disappeared as soon as he realized what was happening. Within a few minutes Pa called him over and told him as he wouldn't be allowed in the studio during recording, he might as well make himself scarce for four or five hours.

I stared at him, shocked. I was playing a whole session and recording with professionals, and one of the greatest musicians of his genre – my Pa? This wasn't kid's stuff and I broke out in a sweat.

"Your guy has bullied me into letting you try your luck on keyboards at a recording session. I hope one of us knows what they're doing. I can't tell how you'll react and you've never played on record. Blind leading the blind."

My confidence suddenly evaporated. He was right. I might be an embarrassment. Then…. to hell with it. I couldn't disintegrate every time I saw him. He'd have to suck it up. I'd do the best I could. He must have seen the steel in my demeanor because he loosened up and said:

"There's a practice room over here. We'll go through a few chords then you can take it from there. The most difficult thing when you're new, is to take note of what everyone else is doing. And even more important…" and he laughed "…is to take notice of what I'm telling you. Doing your own thing when others can't, will do nothing to hide your connection. I'll shout at you as I would all the rest. Understand? Shit, I'll probably shout at you more so don't cry."

"You must be thinking of someone else. I'll try not to shout back."

"Even worse," he said, although there was laughter in his eyes.

We did as he suggested and practiced a bit. Soon I found myself sitting at a baby-grand at one side of a group of casually dressed but serious looking musicians. They noticeably sat up straight when Pa walked in, for all the world like a class of high school students.

The one Pa had called Steve was sitting on a stacking chair, one leg crossed over his knee, drinking coffee and looking a bit put-out.

Pa had covered all bases. If I fouled up, there was someone to step in. My confidence took a nose-dive but this was his world, and he'd been good enough to let me into it.

He motioned me to stand up and introduced me to the rest of the band. I said hello, scarlet with embarrassment. Faces looked up at me curiously, then they said their hellos as if they'd done it a million times before. Which I supposed they had. Pa motioned for me to sit.

The first couple of numbers were fairly light on the piano, although Steve still watched me like a hawk, looking surprised at my competence.

"You played with a band before?" he asked tentatively.

"Only one playing university gigs. Sort of reimbursed amateur. Although the 'reimbursed' bit might hit the skids if I foul up."

He relaxed – probably feeling a bit more confident of his employment.

"You were dragging your bass hand on that last number. Play with the pads of your fingers. This piano'll sound different from those you're used to. The hammers are tacked to soften the tone."

My confidence was restored over time and I had to rein in my enthusiasm. I saw Pa scowling at me from time to time. Eventually he stopped and asked what the hell I was playing as it seemed to be different from everyone else.

He proceeded to play the part I'd done wrong on his guitar. Then he played the whole song from the beginning so I could hear how it all fit together.

Every face was turned towards me, and I could have sunk through the floor. I redoubled my efforts after that and listened carefully to the music as a whole instead of just my bit of it. It was like singing harmony in a choir.

I figured the vocals must be dubbed in on top of the orchestration later, and the two mixed together, although I doubted it was as simple as that. Without vocals it sounded a bit like classical music gone wrong.

I made lots of mistakes, some I knew about, some Pa merely

glared at me for. But I was playing, so time slipped away as it always did.

I did notice one thing. Pa couldn't read music either. He played by ear like I did.

I enjoyed myself so much it was all I could do not to throw my arms round his neck when we left the studio.

Simm was waiting in the car out front. My glowing face told him all he wanted to know. Pa leaned against the wall next to the door and lit a cigarette as if otherwise occupied, but he looked away and gave a half-smile as we sped off.

We stayed at Connie's overnight then set off back home to Ginsling early.

Maurice had moved his belongings into the cottage. He and his teenage kids were in the process of putting things away when I put my head round the door.

"Need anything?" I asked.

"No thank you, Miss Christina. We've plenty of room and have brought food to last us a few days."

He looked at his kids, two girls. Both with hair as long as mine. One was very tall, slim and blonde and the other a red-head, a skinny live-wire. Early teens, I would guess. Neither looked as if Maurice could have produced them. Perhaps he hadn't.

"Stand up girls. This is Miss Christina."

He would have smoothed their hair and pulled down their t-shirts if he could. He gave very little away, but I could see he was immensely proud of them.

"This is Betty," he said placing his large hand briefly on the curls of the smaller one, "and this is Carolyn." She cuddled up to his arm, overcome by shyness.

"Can I have a patch of soil?" asked Betty. "I like to make gardens. I won't make a mess."

Grace would have loved her. Perhaps I should put her in charge of the rhododendrons.

"Quiet, Betty," said her father formally. "Don't bother Miss Christina at the moment - she's probably tired from her journey."

Things were going to have to change around here. This 'Miss Christina' thing for a start. I'd never live it down.

Could this be the lunk who'd blacked my eye? Ed had a lot to answer for.

"Well, just shout if you need anything," I said and went to join Simm.

Gil called that evening. He was very excited by the session - he'd loved my work – *work?* – he said. He'd like to use – *use?* – me again. Music-speak, I supposed.

"But if you think this is leading to stage work, you're mistaken. I wouldn't wish my life on my worst enemy."

"No-one need know who I am. I could legally change my name… I could marry Simm!"

My beloved's face was a picture. I felt immediately guilty and hung my head in shame.

"I'm so sorry - that was awful," I said, dismayed.

Simm meanwhile, had recovered, and was grinning broadly.

"What a great idea – I'd never have thought of it."

"Liar. You bought me an engagement ring!"

"Hello…HELLO," yelled Gil down the phone. "Anyone there?"

"I give up – I truly give up," I groaned. "I only want to play music and now I've a father who wants me to do anything but, and a boyfriend who wants me to be a housewife. I slapped the phone in Simm's hand and said:

"Here – you sort it out."

I should have known better, I really should. Within fifteen minutes they were choosing the hymns.

Chapter Four

An Invitation and World War Three

Christie

They said they'd been joking about the hymns. The hell they were!

When Gil finally got around to the purpose of his call – apart from telling me I was the new Thelonious Monk – I was so delighted I jumped up and down.

He and Giulia had invited us to their home in the Colorado mountains for a December house party.

I gathered it was Gil who usually put a spoke in the wheel when it came to visitors, so we felt suitably honored. A few close friends were welcome, but family and music people were strictly forbidden. As Gil put it:

"They're a pain in the ass and they interrupt my tranquility." Poser!

Gil, Giulia, Jamie, Connie and I all had December birthdays. Jamie and Connie weren't in the picture which left three of us to celebrate.

Gil invited Harry Forster, David Ellis and partners. We'd be staying for a week mid-month with plenty of time to get back to our various homes for Christmas.

I had an absolute ball in the meantime, spending Simm's money on gifts, more glitzy than expensive. We visited every shop in LA, or so it seemed, and filled the car to the roof with multi-colored parcels.

"No need for trees or greenery," said Giulia unnecessarily when I phoned to thank her and ask if there was anything she'd like me to bring. "I thought we might have an early Christmas Dinner as a celebration."

"Good idea." I said, thinking it might get me out of endless cooking on the twenty-fifth.

"You might like to bring a turkey," she continued. "Gil reckons he's going to get a license to kill a wild one but there're two things against that. One, he might not find one, and two, he'd probably decide at the last minute they are beautiful and don't deserve to go in the oven. I can't see him gutting or plucking one either."

"No, I can't picture him sitting in an apron covered in turkey blood and feathers either," I said. "Potatoes, greens, carrots?"

"Oh yes. Thank you. I'll get some cranberries. I like making cranberry sauce." The whole shebang then.

"See you Wednesday." I could imagine her smiling down the phone before she put down the receiver but, of course, I couldn't see.

So, we arrived at 'Mon Repose' – who the hell would call a house 'Mon Repose'? – that Wednesday afternoon.

There were five inches of snow on the dirt road from the highway. Fortunately, Simm had put snow chains on the tires. The long driveway to the house had been cleared, and the trees and bushes strewn with colored fairy lights.

Just inside the gates was what I could only describe as a 'gingerbread cottage' with flickering lights, must be candles and lots of them, inside. Gil stood on the doorstep in a parka with the hood up, holding an acoustic guitar. I wished I'd had a camera.

"Want some help with the candles?" I asked wryly.

"Oh great! I was hoping you'd ask."

We both hopped out of the car, went inside, took a deep breath and proceeded to blow out about a hundred candles. Gil used a candle snuffer and managed twice as many as we did together. Smart ass!

"Get in and drive, Simm. I've been shoveling snow all afternoon so you can get to the house."

He got in the front passenger seat so I was relegated to the back."

"You have not...I don't believe you," I pouted.

"On the button, *Querida*. That day'll never come."

He punched Simm on the arm hard enough to leave a bruise and said:

"Hey, man. How've yer bin? It's going to be a great week with all you guys around. I feel it in my bones."

I rather thought Simm felt it more.

The house was something else. A huge, glass gabled wall to the front reflected back a myriad twinkling fairy lights. There were half a dozen young fir trees, still growing from the soil, decorated to within an inch of their lives with baubles, tinsel, snow (fake, I thought or...perhaps not?) and, surprisingly, popcorn garlands threaded onto string.

Indoors, Giulia stood in the middle of festive debris wearing a Santa hat and looking for all the world like an elf. She was engrossed in threading a glittery streamer of ivy round the door jamb, but it kept unpeeling.

Gil took it from her and forced it into the gap above the door where it stuck fast.

"Thank you, darling," she said and stretched as tall as she could to kiss him on the lips. His eyes crinkled at the corners.

"Hello, my little sugar plum fairy" and he tweaked her on the nose. The hat slid over one eye and she pushed it back again.

"Hi there, Christie. Welcome to the Robson Christmas and Birthday Madhouse. Here, drape this over the tree."

She handed me an impossibly long string of red shiny beads and indicated the mother and father of all Christmas trees which stood to the side of the enormous window.

"Come with me, Christie – I have something to show you." said Gil softly, returning the beads to Giulia.

He helped me into coat and boots, and we climbed the steep banking behind the house, our footprints black indentations in the blinding snow.

At the top, spread before us was a panorama of silver-white, unmarked as far as the eye could see. Beyond, row upon serried row of the Colorado Rockies, deeply shadowed in purple, their tips struck with violet and a pink so pale it appeared translucent in the setting sun. It was the most beautiful sight I had ever seen.

"Just wait," said the gentle voice of my Pa behind me. "The best is yet to come."

The giant orb of the sun slipped further and further to the horizon. When sun touched snow there was an explosion of light, which burst into fire across the sparkling ridges and edged each nook and cranny with purest gold.

I stepped back in awe, and my Pa's arms steadied me. He kissed my hair and whispered:

"It never ceases to amaze me. It's the most spectacular sight in the entire world."

I couldn't disagree.

I pushed away and stood alone - I couldn't tear my eyes away. Slowly the sun's disc sank below the horizon, deepening the shadows, and one by one the stenciled ridges disappeared into the twilight. It had been a glorious revelation.

I stood quite still for some time. When I turned it was to see another sight which left me just as breathless. My Pa was gazing down at me with such love it took by breath away. But the name he whispered was 'Connie'. I must have looked so like her silhouetted against the mountain vastness.

Pa didn't see her, but I became aware of Giulia standing behind his shoulder, the Santa hat still in her hands. She looked distraught, but she straightened her shoulders, pasted on a smile and went back indoors. This poor woman had been doing the same for most of her life.

I went back to the house with Giulia, but Pa leaned back against a snow-laden pine, deep in his own thoughts.

I momentarily turned to see him walk away, never taking his eyes from the fading sunset.

Harry and Barbara, the girl he'd met first in Austin and then at Champaign University when he'd been tailing me, arrived at that moment. It distracted Giulia and she did a pretty good job of greeting them under the circumstances.

They both pitched in to finish the tree, and just as Harry was reaching up to fix the star, Davy arrived trailing a very overwhelmed teenager, much the same age as me.

"This is Mary" he said, parked her on a chair in the corner and went to help Giulia finish up. Jeez, sometimes I hated men!

I sat with her. She was only a year younger than me, but she made me feel old. She giggled tearfully, totally out of her depth. I motioned Simm to come sit with her for a while. I'd noticed something else. Pa was missing.

I felt inclined under the circumstances to take Giulia's side. He didn't deserve consideration when he didn't give it in return. Our mutual delight in that natural wonder and his reaction to me, somehow seemed irrelevant when he was so repeatedly cruel, so insensitive. So I left him to his own devices.

"Come on, everyone. Who's up for a snowball fight?" I said, to lighten the mood.

"Oh, please don't. Gil will have a heart attack. He so loves the peace here and you will make so much noise," Giulia pleaded.

By this point in time, I didn't care what Gil thought. He'd thoroughly pissed me off. Pa or no, rock star or no, he'd to consider Giulia's feelings at least some of the time.

I fetched everyone's coats and dropped them on the floor next to the outside door.

"If you don't join me, I'll spend the evening lobbing snowballs at the door and shouting swear words. Noise will be made. You choose who makes it."

All except Giulia put on their coats and ran, laughing, out into the snow which had gained another couple of inches since we arrived. It was dropping from an inky sky and floating to earth in soft feathers. I loved this weather.

Giulia stood on the top step, silhouetted against the bright lights indoors, jumping from one foot to the other in consternation.

She was so distressed I walked back, helped her into her coat and dragged her into the snow. She protested every inch of the way. He'd so much to answer for – she seemed terrified of offending him.

"If he complains I'll tell him to go to hell and march him there personally," I blustered.

I thought my bravado might buoy her up but it didn't and soon she was back on the top step. At least, this time, she was wearing her coat.

Meanwhile Davy, Harry and Barbara had stockpiled snowballs so when I turned round, I was splattered from head to foot.

"Right!" I yelled, "this is war!"

I didn't look very war-like as I zipped behind the nearest tree for cover while I collected ammunition of my own. At that moment I was joined, ducking and diving by Simm and Mary.

It was then I knew we'd easily win. This was Simm's kind of thing.

The three of us hurriedly made our own snowballs and, carrying an armful each, crept after Simm who put his finger to his lips for silence. We tiptoed between the trees, our footsteps deadened by the deep snow.

We reached our destination and the battle began in earnest. Mary caused surprise and consternation amongst our opponents by being a dead shot, getting Barbara clean in the middle of the forehead.

The laughter got louder and louder, and it ended up with Simm wrestling Davy to the ground and rubbing snow in his face.

Whatever protests Giulia was shouting were drowned out by sheer exuberance. We all stood round the two figures struggling in the snow, shouting out support or feigning surprise, shaking hands and doing high-fives, losers and winners alike.

Until Mary picked up another fistful of snow and lobbed it hard at Barbara, who was ready for her this time, and ducked.

There was a yell which could have started an avalanche. The snowball had hit a furious Pa square on the ear. He pulled himself up to his full height and roared:

"What the fuck do you think you're doing? You were invited here because I thought I could trust you not to defile my home. Get off the ground, get your belongings and fuck off. You're not welcome here."

He stomped back across the virgin snow to the rear of the house and disappeared amongst the trees.

Chapter Five
A Hard Lesson Learned

Christie

Giulia stood cowering. I'd been pretty pissed at him before but this was too much. Just who did he think he was? God Almighty? I'd sort this bastard out once and for all.

It's difficult to push your sleeves up with three layers of clothing underneath, but I had a damn good try.

"Stop!" I yelled. "Fucking stop, you son-of-a-bitch. I have something to say to you."

I missed him in the dark and couldn't make out his footsteps in the snow, but within a few hundred yards he stepped out from behind a tree looking like a prize fighter.

"What was all that crap up there?" he sneered, pointing to the top of the rise we'd stood on to watch the sunset. "You didn't understand a single thing you saw. Don't call me Pa again, ever."

He turned to resume his walk through the snow but I grabbed his arm. Arrogant bastard! I'd absolutely had it. I did something I'd never done before in my whole life – something I never thought I was even capable of – I pulled off my glove, threw it in the snow at my feet and hit him as hard as I could across the face. He almost fell with the force of the unexpected blow. I guessed the last person to do that to him had been his bully of a father when he'd been a small child.

I ran back to the house and stamped the snow from my boots. Pushing Giulia out of the doorway, I threw my belongings into my bag and ran down the icy steps.

If Gil wanted silence, he now had it by the bucketful. No-one dare move.

"You can do as you like Simm," I said, "but make up your mind now because I'm taking the first flight back to Los Angeles. I jumped in the car, keyed it and it started at the second attempt.

Simm didn't even have time to collect his things before I stormed off down the drive. I don't know what I left behind outside the house, but later I assumed it must have been something of a car wreck.

I was so furious I heard nothing but the drumming of my heart until we pulled into the parking lot at the airport.

"Well, that's torn it," said Simm. "You do great bridge burning."

"I didn't burn the bridge – he did, the son-of-a-bitch. He can go to hell. I never want to see him again."

"Only playing devil's advocate here, Christie, but you and your Pa have started a ball rolling neither of you will be able to stop. When you come down, you're going to hate yourself as well as him."

I would not cry. I absolutely would not cry.

"I can't let him treat us all like that," I sobbed. "What else would you have me do?"

"Bear in mind they were his friends much longer than they were yours. His wife and friends spent years keeping you safe for him. Don't throw their efforts in their faces."

Shit, I felt awful. Every word he'd said was true.

"I think it might be an idea to try and pry out the underlying problems and see if they can't be fixed. It seems to me Gil finds this impossible so perhaps he needs your help.

"He always goes off the deep end and becomes over-emotional before anything useful can be done. You're the opposite. You keep at it long after everyone else has given up the ghost. Could be your Pa does need your help."

Simm's calm manner had begun to bring me back down to earth. Perhaps Pa and I were cut from the same cloth. We both lost our tempers, but it upset him beyond reason whereas it made me determined to have my own way, that was true.

Looked at like that, it would seem I had the upper hand. I wondered how Pa was taking it.

"You told him you were flying to Los Angeles so he'll think you're heading for San Clemente. That's the way you always go," said Simm.

"I doubt he'd think far enough ahead to get there. He'll expect me to go to him."

"Then you'll have to find some way to compromise. For your own peace of mind you really do have to sort this out before it goes any further."

The thing about Simm was he was almost always right. That can be annoying but it can also be very comforting. I was so grateful to him. His grandmother's death had been a disaster for him, yet here he was trying to sort out my problems."

"After the last upset, he ended up at Jamie's grave," I mused. "But there are reasons for him not to return there. I don't know; I'll have to think about it. He'll be with someone he feels at ease with, or a place which brings back happy memories. Not many options on either front."

"Do you mind me making a suggestion?" said my wonderful man. "Why don't you call Giulia and ask her where he is. If he's not home, someone might be able to guess where he went."

I called an obviously devastated Giulia.

"I take it he's gone?" I said, stiffly. Giulia sobbed on the other end of the line.

"Can I come and speak to you and anyone else who's still there?" I asked. "I've caused this unholy mess - I have to try and help put it right."

I was back at Pa's house as quickly as I'd disappeared.

"Can you think of anywhere he might have gone?"

This was the second time I'd had to go chasing after him in case he did himself grievous bodily harm. The thought didn't make me sympathetic - it made me mad as hell with him all over again.

"What about seeing Jamie's grave – like last time?" suggested Harry.

"Please trust me on this. There are things I can't tell you but I know he won't be there." My right of passage – I'd started speaking from Dad's script.

I couldn't tell them Gil and I were regularly in touch with Jamie and had talked to him a couple of times. They'd have us locked up.

David turned to Harry.

"You don't think it's possible he might have gone up to the cabins at Anasazi again, do you?"

"No. He went there once before. I'd be surprised if he went back to the same place twice."

"What about the Teacher?" asked David.

"Who?" I said. He sounded like someone out of Star Wars.

"He's the teacher at our spiritualist church. Gil was especially close to him before his move to Colorado. But the problem is, if Gil asked him not to say where he was, there's no way he would break a confidence," David said.

"Worth a try though, I guess. If he recognized Gil's distress he might be persuaded," said Harry.

Harry called Daniel Jones but he said it was quite a while since he'd seen Gil and even then he'd left without saying goodbye. That Harry was so worried did communicate itself to him, and although he couldn't actually tell them where he was, if they left a number he'd get back to them if he heard anything.

"You don't suppose he could have gone to Crestone?" asked David, looking at Harry.

Harry, David and Gil had come across an unusual retreat on a ride in the mountains, where Gil appeared to have some kind of revelation. It had given him a new outlook on life, even clearing away the last of his addiction problems. That sounded a possibility, but then David reconsidered:

"That's a problem because its high in the mountains and we can only reach it on horseback. We won't be able to hire mounts until the morning" said David to Giulia. "I don't suppose you keep horses here?"

She shook her head.

"Then we'll rest and be off first thing," confirmed Harry.

The story of their day I heard later. It was a tale of failure and distress for a friend Harry had cared so much for, he'd helped protect his daughter for years.

They slept fitfully and were awake and ready to go by five o'clock. They didn't stop for breakfast but Giulia, who looked as if she'd been awake all night, had fixed them something to eat on the journey and filled water bottles for them.

It was an easy drive half of the way, then a dirt road to the site of the ruined studio. They picked up horses on the way there, although the stable owner wasn't happy to lease them owing to the uncertain weather. Finally they paid up-front and left the SUV for surety. From there it was only a couple of miles to Anasazi.

They tried to ride past the ruins without looking. It had been a happy place full of youthful memories of friends long gone from their lives. Now the studio was blackened and stark against a frosty sky. The cabins, once so full of life, had missing roofs or broken windows. In some places, the log walls had disintegrated and lay in humps under the snow. Gone, forgotten.

The road through the mountains to Crestone, the site of the spiritual community, a haven for many sects, became increasingly deep in snow until the horses were almost to their knees. David and Harry dismounted and tried to wade their way through, leading the horses as they went, but the sparkling blanket just got deeper and deeper.

There came a point where they had to admit the way was impassable and they'd have to turn back. But if they hadn't been able to get through, they reasoned, perhaps Gil hadn't either. They had to hope for the best.

They returned disconsolate to the house at Riverside.

I'd seen Harry and David leave. I hadn't been able to sleep either and looked out of the window in time to see the lights of David's SUV disappear down the drive as they left. I couldn't believe Gil would do this again. He hardly knew me - I couldn't be responsible. There had to be something else. I cursed him under my breath.

Giulia was exhausted so I sent her off to rest, even if she couldn't sleep. I told her I would call her immediately if there was any news.

Breakfast was a bleak affair of coffee and toast, neither of which I tasted. I returned to the window in the cathedral room which looked to the mountains and prayed to them for help to find someone who loved and understood them so well. Then it hit me.....

That was it! He understood them. He never would have gone trailing down treacherous snow-covered mountain roads on a fruitless journey.

An early winter twilight had begun to dim the landscape, but the snow had stopped. There would be no footsteps to follow but I turned on a torch and walked up the path to the rear of the house. I turned the light this way and that, searching for clues. Nothing.

I climbed higher up the hillside, resting occasionally because of the steepness of the climb.

The last glow of the failing sun lit the horizon but this time, I didn't turn to watch.

I ploughed on, higher and higher, trying to maintain a straight line so I could easily retrace my steps. Still no sign.

The trees threw dark shadows across my path and occasionally an overburdened branch plopped snow from above.

I'd come to the top of the slope, and the ground had become flat and the walking easier - until my foot slipped into a hidden drift and I was stuck, one leg deep in the snow and the other knee wedged against rock. I put out my hands to try and save myself and the torch skittered across the snow out of sight. I was stuck fast and helpless in the pitch dark.

I tried to extricate myself but the more I struggled the deeper I sank and the tighter my knee lodged against rock. I daren't fall backwards or forwards for fear I might not get up again and would suffocate beneath the snow.

There was only one thing to do. I filled my lungs with pure mountain air and screamed for help. My voice echoed amongst the trees and down towards the valley below. I had climbed too far from the house for them to hear me and it was clear Pa wasn't here.

I yelled again. The snow, wet from my body heat, began to melt against my leg. My salopettes had ripped in the fall and slowly the water penetrated to my skin. It burned like hell for a while then my leg became numb and I couldn't feel anything.

I started to get drowsy, and my cries became weaker. I knew I had to fight to stay awake. In the end I couldn't call at all and I knew I was finished.

Just as I was about to give up hope and was drifting in and out of consciousness, peaceful and serene, I heard a voice. It took a while for my foggy brain to work out it was Harry. I made a final, super-human effort and weakly shouted

"Here!"

I heard the loud crunching of snow in my right ear and I was freed from my prison. Arms lifted me and tucked me inside a parka for warmth. This wasn't Harry who was delicate to the point of femininity. These were strong, capable arms.

I briefly opened my eyes and found myself gazing up my Pa's nose. Fortunately, I blanked again at that point.

Chapter Six

Building a Future

Christie

When I came to, I was laying on the floor in front of a roaring fire in Giulia's little sitting room. My every muscle and bone screamed in agony as the blood began to flow. Pa was kneeling at my feet rubbing them hard between his hands, but I couldn't feel a thing. Giulia had hold of one hand and Harry the other, Simm was kissing my forehead, tears rolling down his unshaven chin.

Oh boy, things must be bad if Simm was crying. He was the eternal optimist. He could always find a rosy side.

"Get some pain killers!" yelled Pa to no-one in particular. Simm dropped my head and ran. At least my head hitting the rug distracted me momentarily from the rest of my aches and pains.

"The color's coming back," said Pa, relieved. "Grab that blanket, David and wrap her feet in it."

Instant grabbing and wrapping.

My fingers took longer but I could see them become gradually red and raw which at least meant there was blood in them. All I could think was 'Thank God, I'd be able to play piano again'.

Funny how your mind reverts to banalities when your body has come close to giving out.

I was given a couple of pain killers and, swathed in blankets like a baby, carried to bed by a grim-faced Pa. He laid me down with infinite care and pulled the coverlet over me. I heard Simm's voice drift from far away.

"I understand if you want me to go. This is your tragedy and Christie's. You need to sort it yourselves."

I assumed he'd gone because I didn't hear him again.

When I woke, Pa was kneeling at the bedside holding my hand, fast asleep and snoring gently. I tousled his hair and noted, with passing interest, it was beginning to thin.

We had such an affinity. Despite what he'd said in anger, he knew I understood the sunset and shared how it felt. I'd said things I regretted too, and my whole body physically squirmed when I remembered the slap across his face.

At the movement, he stirred and began to wake. The minute I saw his face I knew he hadn't moved away from me since he placed me on the bed. He struggled for words then simply said:

"I'm sorry."

He examined my face for my reaction.

"Can I call you Pa again?"

"Nothing else, ever," he said.

"We need to talk – big time, Pa. There are so many things to thrash out. Things far beyond you and me."

He agreed, resigned - he'd come to that conclusion himself.

"You'll need your strength. I'll go get you some food," he fussed.

"Before you go, just where did you get to when you left?"

"I went to hear Jamie again. This time at Anasazi where I'd heard him in the mountain snows before. I don't hear him anymore since he took up with you," he said, sounding a bit irritated. "He must have been there because there was suddenly no doubt in my mind, I had to put things right with you. He gave me a real kick in the butt!"

Tears had sprung to his eyes. He wiped them away and disappeared out of the door. He was just so lonely. Perhaps that was the problem or at least part of it, and it had been even worse for him than for Connie."

When the door opened again, it was Simm with a tray full of food. Ham and two eggs, buttered toast, freshly-squeezed orange juice and a steaming coffee press.

"I was cold – not dying of hunger," I remarked.

"I know," he said ruefully, "but your Pa kept piling stuff on the tray. You started off with ham, one egg and coffee. All the rest is him."

"Jeez, I hope he doesn't intend going over the top with the conversation we're about to have. I might as well just go and jump off the roof now."

Just my luck - he walked in as I spoke.

"I promise not to be an ass," he said. "Well not to you any way."

"What do you think is the best way to tackle this?"

The question was to Pa but Simm chipped in instead, an altogether better idea.

"Do you mind me interrupting, Gil?"

"No, he doesn't," I answered for him.

"See you've started the way you mean to go on," he grinned at me. "I'd eat something if I were you, Gil. You're the one who'll need all their strength."

"Well?" I said pointedly.

"I think you should sit down with pencil and paper and decide what the problems you need to tackle are. You mustn't shy away from things just because they're difficult. It's time to face the music. If you aren't prepared to be thoroughly - even brutally - honest with each other, you might just as well quit now. You've used up eight of your nine lives, Gil. This is your very last chance to get back on track."

"That'll do for now, Simm," I said firmly, as Pa was turning an interesting shade of green. "We'll figure it out and keep you up to date as we go along."

"Right, Cap'n!" he said, and saluted. Oh for heaven's sake.

Chapter Seven

Rules, Regulations and Departures

Gil

If I could have chosen anyone on earth for a daughter, it would have been Christie. I used to think it would be Giulia. Perhaps it once was.

Christie was smart, funny, kind and so strong. Strong in a way I once was, but never could be again –I was just worn out. Sometimes she was too forthright, but that was her way.

So when I knew the time came for brutal honesty, there was just nobody I'd rather have had by my side. She might tear me to pieces with her principles – God knows, I probably deserved it – but she would defend me to the last breath of her body to the rest of the world.

And she had become as much a part of me as the midnight skies of Colorado or the towering mountain peaks. And as much a wonder.

I sometimes pondered why my guiding spirit had left it so late in life for me to find her.

She sat with her head on one side in contemplation, looking at me shrewdly. Mouth full, she offered me some toast and a drink of her coffee which I took.

"Did you realize when you stopped thinking of yourself and were worried about me, your own problems receded. That's something you should take serious note of."

It was true. I was so desperate to find her safe I never even noticed I was cold. In fact, I think I could have walked stark naked through the snow until I found her safe. I saw what she was getting at, but if I was brutally honest, I had to admit I was as worried for my own sanity as I was for her safety. I wondered if all fathers were like that with daughters.

"Your profession has made you pandered to and waited on since your teens. You could have any woman you wanted by crooking your finger – even at fifteen which I'm sure you must agree was unhealthy. You have money to burn. That's not your fault. It's a side effect.

"But God alone knows how that poor woman in there has suffered you for so long. You ache for Connie – have done since you were eighteen – yet you deserted each other when you should have been trying to work things out."

Shit, this was painful and we'd hardly started. As all the sins were mine, it could only get worse. I owned up to her truth.

"Put your mind to some solutions before we continue. I'm going to write this down so you remember exactly what you've agreed to. Get me a pen and paper," she said with a furrowed brow.

I did as I was told.

"One," she scribbled and waited.

"I should find something useful to spend my money on," I said, ashamed. "Some charity?"

"No. You can't buy your way out of this. It must be something you're obliged to give time and effort to.

"Two.... "

"I should sort out my treatment of Connie and Giulia."

"Priority. Three…"

"I should stop playing the field. You don't know how hard that is for me being on the road. I get lonely," I pleaded.

"See, all 'me' again. How about giving some consideration to the poor deluded souls who think you're God? Doubtful, but there's an outside chance they might rethink their ways. Anyway, it'd improve your self-respect."

I must have looked shell-shocked because she stopped writing and said:

"That's enough for now. Go think about solutions and we'll start again tomorrow. I'm going to fix you something to eat."

Christie jumped out of bed, eager to get on, now there was finally something to get on with.

She handed me her notes. This was a walk in the mountains situation.

I ate, kissed her on the forehead and noticed for the first time ever, that someone's thoughts had been entirely for me. I had been so mired in my own troubles I'd never even noticed. It must have often been the case but I had never seen it. It was a sobering thought.

Harry, David, Barbara and Mary had already left. Giulia and Simm were having a serious conversation.

"We're going to San Clemente," said Giulia. "To give you some space."

I could see she was struggling so I sat beside her, kissed her affectionately on the lips and said:

"Are you sure you're okay with that? I want you to know I'll be thinking of you."

She looked at me quizzically. I realized with horror it was the first time I'd considered her feelings in a long, long time.

Christie's efforts must be taking effect already.

After they'd gone – Giulia looking so despondent – Christie was behind me, holding my parka and snow-boots. She was smiling encouragingly, quite unconscious of having read my mind – again.

"Thank you for taking this seriously," said my darling as I hugged her.

"Thank you for caring about my life," I replied, entirely sincere.

"You're my Pa. What else would I do?" she said simply.

I strode through the still of the mountain vastness until I was tired, then took her paper from my pocket and studied it. Noticing it was in her own writing was profoundly comforting. She was giving of herself without wanting anything in return. Perhaps I wasn't as adrift as I'd thought.

I looked out across the sparkling sunlit expanse, and realized it made me feel microscopic. I'd felt like that before – gazing down across the cabins of Anasazi. Perhaps, despite everything, it was a part of the spirit I clung to for my sanity's sake.

I breathed deeply of the cleansing air, looked to the sheer immensity of the sky and sighed. I knew my calm was about to be shattered, as I skimmed through Christie's notes.

I needed to find a way to spend my millions usefully. I was still selfish enough to want it to have meaning for me too. Perhaps I could help support a charity – that would be meaningful, but Christie had warned me against trying to buy myself out of my problems. My efforts would have to be placed elsewhere. I could sing. But who to? I'd see if Christie had any ideas.

The celibacy on tour thing could be a problem. But I took her point about groupies. There were 'professionals' who followed the band around from place to place but they were few, so easy to avoid. The majority were star-struck little girls who for a few moments just wanted to be the center of attention for their heroes.

47

Girls like my Christie. I would kill with my bare hands any man who tried that with her. Jamie and Ed had disgusted me in the past. I realized now I'd felt much the same about myself.

When I'd had to admit what I'd done to Connie, I was mortified. But that hadn't stopped me. I continued to do exactly as I pleased. That was the beginning of the end for us. All my fault.

But consideration of Connie and Giulia had to be the last thing, I realized. I needed to make peace with the rest of my life before I could help with theirs. And of course eventually all three of us would have to talk it out face to face. Oh God, a replay of the meeting with Oliver. The bottom went out of my stomach.

The days turned into weeks and my catalogue of horrors unfolded. They were interspersed with Christie's small flaws. She'd smoked pot with a boyfriend and lied to Julius and Cathy, she'd listened in to an argument between Grace and Connie and such like. All teen misbehavior shared by everyone her age. Even Julius and Cathy would have laughed it off. And I? I cringed.

Chapter Eight
A Meeting of Minds

Giulia

I'd never been to San Clemente before. Strange when I'd travelled the whole world and only lived sixty miles away in Los Angeles for almost all my life.

I'd known Gil through my brother Larry and I loved him from the moment I set eyes on him. He was kind and endlessly patient with an awkward teen who habitually said the wrong thing.

As I grew older, I would watch him bent over Larry's prized guitar, demonstrating chords my brother fluffed time and again. Always he was patient, always non-judgmental.

I was eight years old. Naturally, I didn't know I loved him. He was ten years older than me. A man when I was a child. But what is true at eight may not be at eighteen. When his marriage to Connie began to fail, I watched all his agonies, unable to help. He would have pushed me away.

I watched him get high with help from my father. Saw him in rehab when he'd become dependent on cocaine, watched him get falling-down drunk and roar at the unfairness of it all. I knew how to fix it but I couldn't tell him.

Then Jamie died and he with him. He was a walking dead man for years. The only thing keeping him tethered to this earth was his music and the friends in his audiences. He went back to the drink and drugs, even spoiling shows with his behavior. Then, of a sudden, he seemed to pull himself together.

It was a combination of two things, I think: the horror he'd let down the only friends he'd confidence in, his audience, and Christie's birth. He'd to live to find her. I never saw such determination in a man before or since.

49

But it cost him. He turned in on himself to survive, though I wasn't disappointed when he turned his back on most of his former life.

And all the time there was Connie. As I had loved him, so he'd loved Connie. And there was no end to it. They had gone through an appallingly destructive divorce, They seemed to be on a roller coaster neither could get off.

Connie tried. She committed to Oliver and even took his name, although they never married. Had he behaved half-way decently to Gil she probably would be with him still.

Oliver's peculiar jealousy of his son was such that Simm loved Connie with all his heart, and so did his beloved grandmother, Oliver's mother.

And Simm was the reason I had come to San Clemente, while Christie and Gil worked out my future as well as his.

"We can sit here and mope," said Simm, "or we can get on with our lives and try for some distraction."

I wasn't sure what I wanted. My heart and soul were still in our house in Colorado. I gazed at the telephone avidly every time I walked past. But, for the moment, it didn't ring.

Perhaps an afternoon at the beach with Simm would be a temporary diversion - or a visit to the theater. It wasn't so far to the opera in San Francisco.

I mentioned it to Simm as we took breakfast the following morning. We discovered we had a mutual love of Mozart. I'd always kept that to myself. It would be impossible for the daughter of Paul Giordano and the wife of Gil Robson to admit that to the world. I always thought I'd be a laughing-stock.

The thought I might enjoy myself seemed like a betrayal of my husband. I knew he would be put through hell by his daughter.

But I also found sympathy for Christie. Perhaps she could sort out this mess the adults in her life had made. Poor girl. I pitied her. This shouldn't fall on her young shoulders.

I hung around the house that day waiting for a phone call which finally came in the late evening. Gil sounded dreadful. Christie sure wasn't pulling any punches.

The day before they'd talked all day, which was exhausting in itself, then today he'd spent on the mountain as I'd known he would. He would need the solitude to think, although he did something he never did, and took his woes with him. Christie had scribbled down a list of things he'd to think through and which must be rectified before he could move on.

I wondered if I was one of those things. When all this was over, Gil and I would go away somewhere quiet to give him peace and time to recover.

There was a high tide on the beach a couple of days later and Simm asked if I'd mind him calling a couple of buddies to go surfing. He'd love for me to come too.

The more distractions the better. So I told him that would be great, and that I would be more than happy after the upset of the past week, to take some time for myself on the beach.

I took coffee in a flask and lathered in sun cream, sat on my towel and tried to put my troubles out of my mind.

Simm was wearing bright red shorts, so he was quite easy to follow in the water. His expertise came as a surprise. He and his friends were a good bit older than the other kids on the beach, but if anything they were more controlled, more skillful. They rode the curls with ease.

I was shocked to find I was actually enjoying watching them.

Gil had never been a surfer, that was Jamie's thing. He didn't even like the sea particularly so sitting on a beach was something I rarely did any more.

Simm's surfing friends were from Los Angeles. In fact, they lived quite close to my family. They were a similar age to my brothers so it was surprising they didn't know each other. But I rather gathered Darren and Tom spent their entire youth on the beach, so as one of my brothers was into guitars and the other played football, perhaps it wasn't so surprising.

They were nice guys, very like Simm in character – full of fizz. They certainly caught the eye of many girls in their teeny-weeny swim-suits. They were conceited enough to give the occasional wink which made me laugh.

At the end of the afternoon, we packed up and went back to Ginsling House so they could shower and change. I was left alone for a few minutes, so I surreptitiously put in a call to Christie. It was mid-afternoon, a time Gil usually spent on the mountain anyway.

She sounded even worse than Gil had. One by one, she was helping him shoulder problems he'd taken a lifetime to acquire.

"He's okay, I guess. At least not ready for cocaine and Jim Beam again yet."

"Yet?"

"Figure of speech. Please don't be mad at me Giulia but can you not speak to him for a while until he's over the next bit of sort-out. If you offer him sympathy, he'll take it and it'll put him back. I know it's tough on you and I know you'd rather be here but believe me, if you could see the pair of us, you'd know it's tough on us all."

He'd clearly come into the room because her voice increased significantly in volume:

"And we all know what a pathetic worm he is. Doesn't need any help from you to backslide."

Over dinner, Simm waved tickets to the theater in my face and looked very pleased with himself. He was deeply bronzed from the sun and his sapphire eyes sparkled with delight.

"I took out a mortgage on my grandma's house to get these. They're like gold dust."

The show was at an open-air theater just an hour's drive up the coast, but I was disappointed to see the tickets weren't for Mozart but Chopin. I had only a vague recollection of his music from high school. It turned out I had just discovered a new passion.

Once I'd put on my turquoise silk evening dress and donned the delicate suite of diamonds Gil had given me all those years ago, I was beginning to feel much better.

The piano twinkled out melodies I couldn't have imagined. I was mesmerized. During the performance the audience were spellbound. At the end, they stood as one and applauded and applauded. It was thrilling.

On the way out, Simm disappeared briefly and came back with an album of Chopin nocturnes as a gift.

While the music was breathtaking, it would have meant so much more if only I'd been with Gil.

Simm looked at me curiously but didn't say anything. I didn't know if he was upset his grand gesture may have been a disappointment. It could just have been he was missing Christie.

Superficially he was an entertaining and open-hearted companion, but I suspected there was much more to him than that.

When we arrived back in San Clemente, I excused myself and went to my room. I knew this was rude but I needed time to think what to do next.

I had had far too much fun spending time with Simm. I'd laughed my way through our beach day and the theater trip had been amazing.

I needed to get away, but I couldn't go back to Denver or our mountain hideaway. It would ruin any headway Christie had made with Gil.

I could go home to the rest of the Giordanos in Los Angeles, but I couldn't stand the thought of the prying questions, especially from my mother. She would know immediately something wasn't right and hammer away until she had the whole story. I suspected then she'd be at 'Mon Repose' like a shot. No.

Lucy was a trusted friend but she wasn't the type you could share confidences with – it just wasn't her scene.

As far as I could see there was one remaining option and it terrified me.

Connie.

She knew all about everything, and she knew all the people involved well. She knew Simm better than I did by a country mile. But we were both vague about Christie – perhaps we should pool our knowledge.

I called her and asked if she would mind me visiting. I had something to discuss.

She wasn't exactly enthusiastic - why would she be? I couldn't even begin to think how she felt about me. A tiny part of her must hold me responsible for the break-up of her marriage to the man she'd loved almost as long as I had, even if it wasn't true. A man who returned her love.

If honesty was the name of the game, I was going to have to own up to that from the start. This would be a measure of my desperation. If I couldn't fight back, I had to understand.

Chapter Nine

Surprise for Connie from Giulia

Connie

After Giulia's call my knees gave way and I sat down on the sofa with a bump. What the hell was going on? I should be the last person she wanted to talk to. I could only assume it was something vital about Gil.

What had he done now? Hospital, overdose, fallen off a cliff? Perhaps he was…. dead! No, I wouldn't make assumptions - but why couldn't she have told me over the phone?

It was the next day before she arrived. She was very pale and trembling. But she was, thank the Lord, in charge of her emotions.

It was a sad situation.

It seemed that, as soon as the meeting at Windham was over and despite our good intentions, Giulia and I had slipped back to being adversaries again. That darn man had a lot to answer for. He messed up every life he touched, almost always unintentionally.

A tear slipped unbidden down my cheek. Oh, not again – Christie would blow a fuse if I cried.

"Coffee, wine or a stiff drink?" I asked as she took off her jacket and sat down.

"Oh, coffee for now" she replied, "we may need the hard stuff later."

I disappeared into the kitchen, thinking with trepidation that didn't sound promising. What had he done this time? I hadn't yet recovered from his last outburst.

I smiled unconvincingly and placed the coffee on the low table between the sofas.

"I assume it's important for you to contact me. I wouldn't have thought I'd be your first port of call."

"Of course not. If I might get straight to the point?"

I gestured for her to continue as I poured our coffees.

"We had a party for our birthdays at 'Mon Repose' and invited a few friends including Christie and Simm – did you know they were an item?"

"I did - Simm called."

"It's still early days for Gil and Christie – they have a lot to learn about each other. To cut a long story short, they had an appalling argument. Christie was so angry she hit him hard enough across the face to black his eye."

My mouth dropped open.

"She told Gil that she'd had it with him…" Giulia continued.

"At which point, I guess, he completely lost it and bolted." I cursed him under my breath.

Giulia shrugged unhappily. We were both on the point of tears by this point but probably for different reasons.

"Years ago, Harry, David and Gil had ridden up into the mountains from Anasazi," said Giulia, "They came across a religious retreat, where Gil seemed to have some sort of revelation. They thought he might have gone there so they hired horses and set off to try and find him. But it had been snowing quite heavily so they had to turn back."

Damn, he'd frozen to death. She was trying to break it to me gently. I got to my feet and began pacing. He did this to me over and over, the selfish son-of-a-bitch.

"No, don't worry. He's okay, physically anyway." And what did that mean?

"He came home. Distraught, but thankfully okay, but before daybreak, Christie had set off to look for him, blaming herself for the whole mess."

Something had happened to my baby?

"We couldn't see her anywhere, but Harry finally found a set of footprints leading away from the house. They searched through the trees until he heard a faint mewling from further up the hill. Christie had fallen into a drift and had nearly frozen to death.

"Gil bounded up the hillside and carried her back to the house where we managed to revive her."

That was certainly a surprise, Gil was usually too cool to bound anywhere, which said much for his state of mind -

"Fortunately, he'd got to her before she suffered any permanent injury. She slept the clock round but woke in a temper."

Atta girl!

"Damn and she's only known him five minutes. Perhaps we should have done the same."

Giulia look down at her fingers, twisted together on her lap, and nodded miserably.

"And did he raise Cain again? Did he walk out?"

"No. That's the surprising thing. He didn't. He agreed to everything she said. Simm pointed out this was his last chance and Christie told him – to use her expression – if he fucked it up again that was the end. He must have agreed with her."

"So what's the state of affairs now?"

"Christie and Gil are at Mon Repose. Simm and I are in San Clemente at Grace's house. David and Harry went home. Christie won't allow anyone near Gil until she's applied some 'tough love', and she says if anyone visits, he'll play the sympathy card. Then she says they'll be back to square one."

"Oh boy, he sure would. She's right. "

I changed the subject.

"How's Simm. He's a nice boy, isn't he? I'm pleased about him and Christie, but it does feel really weird that my daughter and step-son have hooked up."

"It must. He's fine and doing his best to distract me with occasional success."

I had tried to keep the conversation about them, and not the two of us, but in a sudden rush I said:

"You do realize that one of us is going to be the loser in this, Giulia. Don't you?"

The answer was a forgone conclusion. Giulia was his wife and his help and support for ten years. I had no place in his life. Our marriage had been a catastrophe but I had never let go and never could.

Chapter Ten

The Only Way is Up - Perhaps

Gil

I was just so exhausted. She had hammered away at me for over a week now. She was the only person I saw, and she accompanied me everywhere.

I have to admit I enjoyed our walks though. When I'd accused her of not understanding the mountains, I couldn't have been more wrong. She drank them in - tasted the scent on her tongue, and when I saw their vast expanse reflected in her shining eyes, I knew she was my child.

I did my best singing here - for her. My voice seemed to fly effortlessly through puffs of moisture in the freezing air. The joy it gave her made my heart leap.

But then we went back to the house I was seriously thinking of renaming 'Hell on Earth'.

We talked and talked but we seemed to be making little progress. I just couldn't do some of the things she was demanding.

She insisted I never go back to LA - ever. She conceded my mother was to be an exception, but she must come here and always alone. But Lizbeth and all her connections were not a viability.

That also meant my music career as it stood was at an end.

I completely lost it here. It was the one thing I just could never give up. I was already suffering for lack of my audience friends. I'd taken to writing songs with lyrics – I was lousy at lyrics – and being alone, started to construct music. I tried to play all the instruments myself but came unstuck with the horn and string sections.

Christie said I should do without horns and strings so I looked carefully at my notes. She was right. I could adjust it all - it would work. Harmonies would go unless I over-dubbed my own voice. I could do that too, although I would have to keep it simple. And I would no longer be restricted by band requirements. I could play blues – which I loved – rock n roll even classical if I liked.

Christie said I must learn to fill the gaps. It would give me something to think about. She was tough. But she was right and slowly I began to attempt music I never could have ventured before. It was thrilling – it consumed me.

Then there was travel. Until she – not I – was confident I had everything under control, she would accompany me wherever I went. She understood it wouldn't be pleasant for either of us.

I confess I'd never considered it from her point of view before. It can't have been an exhilarating thought - who, at nineteen, wants to go to a club with their Dad? The thought of clubbing with my own father came to mind and I squirmed.

I hated the very idea I would become a ball and chain. That was an appalling thought, because it immediately made me consider how many other people I'd had dealings with must have thought that way too – band members with family commitments I'd unnecessarily made work overtime, roadies who didn't see their friends and families for months at a time, because I decided to extend a tour. Finally, Connie…. oh hell – Connie who I'd left alone to raise two babies on her own at an age when her social life should have been in full swing.

Shit, what had I done? She'd told me over and over and over how lonely she was. I'd ignored her for the sake of music and friends and just disappeared. I'd been unimpressed when she was so hurt by my association with groupies, when lovemaking should have been hers alone.

I'd put everything before her.

And my mother. I'd relied on her to do what I should have been doing. She'd always spoiled me, and even took in my children when I'd forgotten them, along with my wife. I was an utter fool.

And it had taken my newly discovered daughter to show me these things. She had chosen to do that in the place I felt most at peace, and it was working. Slowly but surely, I was beginning to see faults I hadn't even been aware of, but which other people had had to suffer daily.

I could apologize to all those I had walked over all my life, but that wasn't anywhere near good enough. I felt so inadequate, the same question hammering over and over in my brain. How did I put it right?

There was one thing wrong with all this. It was still 'me' based. What could *I* do, what could *I* say?

There was a natural extension to all this. What had I done to poor Giulia? She had loved me steadfastly all her life, never once wavering in loyalty. Yet I had never hidden the fact that I dreamed of Connie at night, it was Connie I saw when we made love. What kind of monster behaves like that?

A fucking rock star, that's who.

My Dad had been a bastard, but I had to concede he was right about some things. He had sneered at the rich and famous, holding them up as figures of ridicule we should do our damnedest to avoid. Now I was one of them, to my cost. Perhaps if Jamie had listened, my beloved brother might still be alive.

Now one son was dead, and the other – me - was locked in a rock n roll lifestyle, his life in ruins.

And kind, loving Giulia was a member of one of the richest families in Hollywood. How could she ever understand what she was doing? She couldn't even begin to imagine where I had come from – the cruel bullying, the poverty. I was the younger, so I never had anything new, clothes or toys, until my Dad, figuring there was money to be made, bought me a guitar.

Giulia had never known what it was to want anything. Her brother wanted a guitar, her Dad bought him four; her sister wanted to join their father on stage in Vegas, she played a whole season; her brother wanted a pilot's license, his Dad fixed it and lived to regret it. My friend died in a flight accident over Arizona.

The following month Giulia's mother paid for her and her friend to cruise the Caribbean. It didn't bring her brother back, but it was a good distraction. When my brother died, it seemed no-one cared but me and Mom – and Connie.

Christie pointed out for the hundredth time how many 'I's were still in my thoughts, but it had begun to be different. Now it wasn't about how sad I was. It was about what I had done to people I cared about – and those I didn't even know.

Christie said it was a shame I hadn't grown up knowing Grace, Oliver's mother. My life would have been transformed. I must ask her about that sometime.

And then we would walk through the mountain pines again and all my griefs would dispel. Until the next time.

One day I took her to the ruins of Anasazi. I told her about the album Jamie had worked so hard on in the studio there, and how I had been so thrilled for him. When she saw my despondency, she broke off a bit of fire-blackened wood, wrapped it in a tissue and slipped it into my pocket.

I showed her the Snow-line cabin, again full of spider's webs and dirt, but with the remains of my last visit – an empty bean can with traces of dead mold. Where the cabin had been whole on my last visit, some of the shingles had shifted and water had leaked in, rotting the floorboards.

I showed her the rock above the snowline where two grown men had played with snowballs, play-fighting like five-year-olds.

"Well, that should make you feel freakin' guilty at least. You should have joined in our game instead of throwing a tantrum and putting us through even more shit on your behalf,"

She actually sneered at me. How could she unerringly find where to stick the knife?

.

There was just so much crap in my life, but I now knew I wanted it cleansed out of me. Scoured until I was clean again. I said a prayer to the God who had forgiven me, for my Christie.

The final list – I like to think it was arrived at by consensus - ran like this:

If I agreed never to go to LA again for any reason at all, my mother could visit once a month. At her discretion she could bring Jacob and Mylo with her. They could stay for no more than one week.

I would never visit again any place I found stressful or upsetting. They were part of the past and had to be jettisoned and, as far as possible, forgotten.

The playing and writing of music were absolutely encouraged – but alone, at present at least. I was already getting into that. I'd started writing blues songs – these were actually better sung with limited orchestration, and I could do a pretty good job with just my guitar and keyboards. I had help from my daughter with that – it was a pleasure beyond compare to share music with her.

At first my singing of them was pretty poor, but I learned to work with a raw vibrato and repetitive phrasing unique to that style. Christie said at some point she would pass the better ones to record labels. I didn't know that I wanted to.

The next condition went without saying so I was ready for it. There were to be absolutely no drugs, of any kind, within fifty miles at all times. That included cigarettes which I'd to give up immediately – for my health, she said.

She reminded me alcohol was also a drug but conceded that, if I could prove I'd given up smoking, I could have a glass of bourbon every evening.

"You're a sadist," I remarked. She agreed.

"That's the scene, Jimmy Beam!"

I sighed, resigned by this time to my fate.

This looks as if it happened back-to-back. It didn't. It was spread over a period of time, interspersed with putting right the eighteen years of not knowing each other.

Chapter Eleven

Giulia Meets Tom

Simm

It was late when Giulia came back from her meeting with Connie.

I was out on the terrace with a glass of Scotch, enjoying the gentle sea breeze and twinkle of lights along the pier.

I don't know what I'd expected, but she seemed quite composed if a little fragile. She refused the drink I offered and went to bed. I was doing my level best to keep upbeat and sometimes felt I must have looked a complete idiot. No-one in the history of the world had smiled as much as I had over the past couple of days.

The following morning, she skipped breakfast, put on a bikini under her jeans, and set off to find a quiet beach for an early morning swim.

While she was out, I called Christie, just to hear her voice. She must just have come in because she sounded breathless and rushed.

"You can't just call – he knows Giulia's with you. He'll want to talk to her and he can't. I've told her that already but she's soft enough to ignore me - she gives in to him every time. I'll call back at seven."

Then the line went dead.

To fill the time I called Tom Beatty, my surfing buddy, and asked if he'd like to meet me for a beer at Huntington Beach. It'd fill the day and it was obvious Giulia needed space. Things had become decidedly fraught, and I missed Christie to a degree which surprised me.

Tom and I found a beachside bar which overlooked the coastline and drank a beer or two. We had known each other since school so he knew me well enough to understand when something was wrong.

"Spill," he said when I'd remained quiet for a few moments, occasionally hidden behind my beer glass.

"Oh, nothing wrong with me. It's just the whole world around me at the moment. Did you know I was engaged?"

"I heard something of the sort on the grapevine. I was a bit surprised you didn't tell me yourself."

"You are sworn to secrecy Tom, but I'm struggling. My fiancé is called Christie Heywood. Well, that's her adopted name. Her birth name is Christie Robson,"

"Go on…."

"Her natural father is the singer, Gil Robson."

"You're shittin' me!" - I hated that expression - "How is that a problem? Fame, fortune and a certain future. Good deal."

"She only met him a few months ago. They get on like a house on fire. Anyway, the long and short of it is he suffers from severe depression he has a hard time controlling. Christie – not known for her tact - and some of his friends really offended him and he went off the deep end. As a result he disappeared, which apparently is not a rare reaction and usually once found, he's not in a good state. So far, they've got to him in time but recently it's been touch and go.

"At the moment Christie's holed up alone with him at his home in Colorado. She's determined to sort him out one way or another and has banned any visits or communication. I occasionally manage to sneak a phone call but that's all. I can't tell you how much I miss her, Tom."

I took another long drink. I was beginning to feel emotional. I had to snap out of it, so I abruptly changed the subject.

"So, what have you been up to? Booked in for the September gig yet?"

"Giving it a miss. It's not the gas it used to be, too many competitors for the surf and there are often bastards in the crowd who come to cause trouble."

This wasn't working. I had to get the rest of the worry off my chest.

"Tom. You've met Connie, my stepmother? She's Christie's natural mother. She used to be married to Gil. Christie was conceived as their relationship came to an end and Connie hid her from him for eighteen years.

"He was apparently living the rock n roll lifestyle at the time. Anyway, Connie moved in with Dad, Deborah and me, and Gil married Paul Giordano's daughter Giulia. It's tangled like spaghetti!"

Tom had swung round on his chair and was studying me closely.

"Let me get this straight…. you're engaged to your sister? Jeez!"

"Well, no. She's my stepsister so there's no blood link. Connie's my Dad's partner, but has always kept an eye on Christie from a distance - you following this? She had help, believe it or not, from my grandmother, Grace Maxwell who lived near Chicago – she died some years back. Grace couldn't bear to be in the same room with Dad – their relationship has always been acrimonious. She had very good reason for her actions.

"Connie and Grace between them found ways of shielding Christie from Gil, but when she turned eighteen, her foster parents decided she had to be told the full story of her adoption, and the truth came out.

"She's a determined lady, Tom. Sooner or later you'll meet her and you'll see what I mean. I fell for her on sight - she's stunning."

I was beginning to feel overwhelmed by the whole situation and it must have been apparent because Tom continued:

"Would you like me to come back with you? It might be easier with two of us. It'll only be tonight though. I've to be back in LA tomorrow."

I accepted his offer gratefully. It was a temporary measure but would make things easier for a while.

Giulia was at Ginsling House when we got back. She'd just been showered, had her hair wrapped in a towel and a kimono tied round her tiny waist. When she moved, a perfume reminiscent of gardenias drifted in the air.

I couldn't avoid taking stock. She was a beautiful woman – bit flat-chested for my taste but I could understand why Gil had married her. She was sweet-tempered and kind.

She and Connie couldn't have been more different. While Giulia was petite, feminine and needed looking after. Connie was curvaceous, sophisticated and confident. She was also inclined to call a spade a spade without much regard for feelings – a trait associating with Grace had probably not improved.

I would have put Gil with Connie of the two. He definitely needed someone to look after him. There was a certain amount of bitterness in that thought. He was taking up all the time and attention of the two women I loved best.

It was six-thirty and I began to get a bit twitchy about the phone call. I'd told Tom about it, but at the moment, he seemed to be making cow's eyes at Giulia and I couldn't catch his attention.

As neither was aware of my presence at that moment, I quietly sidled into the house and slid the glass windows shut behind me. I unplugged the phone from the coffee table and rehooked it in my bedroom.

It rang dead on seven.

"I can't talk long," she whispered. "He's just got in the shower. He knew I was up to something."

"Are you alright? I worry about you. Gil's not always that predictable."

"I'm fine. We're actually making pretty good progress at the moment. He's admitting to himself what the problems are, and we're making some headway in putting them right. But its hard work because some of the remedies are a bit extreme. Can Giulia hear us?"

For some reason I had copied her whispers:

"No. She's on the terrace being romanced by my friend Tom - he's doing the romancing not her."

"Don't give much for his chances. Gotta go. Call you same time Thursday. Can't ring tomorrow. Apparently, we're going somewhere. Love you, kisses," and she put down the phone. I just wished I could visualize an end to this.

I walked back outside smiling, flinging the windows open as if I hadn't a care in the world.

Giulia was beaming up into Tom's face, and he had an expression I confess in all the years I'd known him I'd never seen before.

This was a potentially explosive situation. I kicked him hard on the shin as I walked past to wake him up.

"Any ideas what to do tomorrow, you two," I said stretching and – surprise, surprise - smiling.

"Tom is taking me to Balboa Park. I lived in LA all my life and have never been. He says there's a terrific art gallery there. I love art galleries."

She smiled naively. Odd how his urgent appointment in LA had suddenly disappeared.

 I don't think I'd have gone as far as to say the art was terrific – it had a smattering of old masters so it was good enough, I supposed.

"Why don't you join us?" asked Tom, looking for all the world as if he'd rather visit the dentist.

"No, sorry. I've a date with Connie – I promised to take her out to lunch."

A little later, when we were on our own, I reminded Tom she was a married woman, and her husband was not too balanced at the moment.

"He's not likely to be around, is he, with Christie on his case?"

Wrong response.

Chapter Twelve

Birth of Redemption

Christie

Some days later, I asked if he'd come to any conclusion about performing his songs. There was a great gaping hole in his plans.

He loved what he was writing. Because I knew it was becoming exceptional – by far the best thing he'd ever done – we needed to get it to an audience. But the music world was made up of shady characters, out for a fast buck. No one knew that better than Gil.

"Does it matter who the audience are?" I said, chewing my lip.

I don't know why I bothered - I already knew the answer. He looked at me as if he couldn't quite believe his ears.

"It has to be the people I've seen month after month, year after year across the foot lights. I've recognized some of them most of my life. It's no exaggeration to say they are my only constant. They're the reason I write music at all."

"Oh right," I said. "*Those* friends."

"How about we build our own venue? Somewhere obscure where only avid fans would want to go?"

"Where could that be?" he frowned then added feelingly. "I could do with a roll-up."

I ignored the last part and went on:

"No idea," I said. This was getting discouraging.

He suddenly sat upright, and a grin spread across his face.

"We'll buy a large piece of land and transform it into an auditorium. We'll build it somewhere obscure – I don't

72

know….in the Mojave – maybe not. We'll figure that later. That'll kill two birds with one stone – expensive and unselfish."

As the plan began to unfold in his mind, he became more and more animated. I could see gaps a mile wide in his proposal, but we could get to them later. At the moment, the main thing was to build on this enthusiasm, give life some sparkle again. I was getting quite excited myself.

My job was to make absolutely certain something came of it.

"I have to find a way to get past those awful blood-suckers who think they're my bosom buddies. Damn, I hate those people. Just one cigarette? Never again?"

"Not the remotest chance." His shoulders slumped.

"Jamie had the best idea. He lied all the time. Every time they asked a question, he gave a different answer. Those he couldn't stomach at all, he flat out refused to have anything to do with. He used to send Lizbeth to tell them he was indisposed."

He laughed out loud at his own memories.

"I think it's a good idea to get rid of those who write downright lies. Disassociate from them altogether. Your fans don't encourage them in any case."

"I'm so used to pandering to them," he said thoughtfully. "I don't think I can."

"Sure you can. And if you can't, I can do a Lizbeth for you."

I could see that that was yet another weight lifted from his shoulders. These so-called experts had formed a barrier between him and his audiences for years.

"Shall I tell you a secret I've never told another soul?" he said doubtfully.

"Go on."

73

He paused still looking reticent, so I lifted my cup and feigned indifference. Then he heaved a sigh of resignation and went on:

"On a couple of occasions, when I've been sick, I've cried off for an extra day and sat in the audience. I went in when it was dark and came out before the end, but I sat through the whole show. I was only recognized once, and when I asked the guy to be quiet, he turned away. It was useful. I could see what was missing and what was good. I could fix things."

I understood what it had cost him to tell a secret he'd felt unable to share with anyone else. So…another bit of cleansing, another tentative step forward.

"Now back to the point. How to get them to you. I like the idea of your auditorium, but you know it would get crashed. Unless you built it here. You could cut down some of the trees on the hillside above the house and have tiered seats cut from the rock. They'd only be small – you can say goodbye to your forty thousand mega-shows. You could arrange security if this is done on land belonging to the house." I paused and thought, then grinned:

"And I have just the guy! Do you know any of your audiences on a personal level?"

"No, not really…. except…a couple over the years, have worked in the band. They'd spread the word tactfully if I asked."

"Well, that's enough for today - you look shattered. We'll talk again tomorrow. Get some sleep."

"No. Tomorrow I have something of my own planned," he kissed my forehead. "Goodnight."

Chapter Thirteen
Nancy Explains

Connie

What Giulia had told me about Christie I found worrying.

Firstly, the obvious thing. She had been injured and I couldn't check she was okay. I'd hate to think she had inherited Gil's self-destruct gene.

Then, she was holed up with Gil who had always been unpredictable. Not for one minute did I believe he would harm a hair on her head, but she was outspoken, and he was over-sensitive – neurotic, even. She could so easily upset him.

And the road she'd taken would be difficult. He would have to face some very unpleasant facts. Could he take it? If anyone could do it, Christie could. I was astounded at how close they had become, and so quickly. But did he care for her enough?

The only thing I could think of to do was to go see Nancy. Did I dare? Could I stop her from hopping the first flight to Denver?

She didn't know about her granddaughter. She was the world's kindest mother, but she was over-protective and that son-of-a-bitch husband of hers was a nightmare to be avoided at all costs.

So going to her house wasn't an option. But I could ask her to come here for a couple of days. It'd be good to see her again. She could bring the boys if she thought it appropriate. They were grown – teens – now and at that age where anything and everything is blamed on parents. In our case, practically anything would probably be true.

How peculiar it was that the bond between he and Christie should have flourished so absolutely. Perhaps he was always meant to have daughters.

I called Nancy. That she was still affectionate at all, I put down to her understanding that Gil probably had to bear more of the responsibility for all that had happened than me. She'd experienced similar loneliness from her family before.

"Hi, Nancy - its Connie. Are you busy or free to talk for a few minutes? Can you come over? I have something to tell you. Best face to face than on the phone."

"Sounds ominous."

"No. But I have to fill you in on some family matters."

"I've nothing else to do - I'll be right over."

"Bring an overnight bag just in case," I suggested.

I made up her bed.

Once a woman's curiosity is piqued, there's no stopping her. If a friend tells you he's going on holiday a man will say 'Mm, that's nice', and a woman's immediate response would be 'Where are you going? Have you been before?' and such like. Nancy was an archetypal woman. I'd told her I had something of note to tell her that couldn't be discussed over the phone, so she was here later the same afternoon.

"Come on in Nancy. So glad to see you - it's been a while."

She hugged me warmly in a way I understood she didn't use with Giulia. That was a shame but there was nothing I could do to build bridges at this late date. It wasn't my place anymore. The most that could be said for me was that I was the mother of her adored grandsons.

"Hello dear. Glad to see you too. Now, what's all this about?"

Nothing like cutting to the chase!

"Let's get you settled first. You can stay? I'd like that - we have some catching up to do."

"Yes, I can. Not to be at Monty's beck and call for a day will be a pleasant change."

"How are the boys? Gil was asking after them when I saw him a few weeks ago," I lied.

The look on her face showed she didn't believe a word of it, but she answered anyway.

"I think you know Jacob is working with Liz, training to be a studio technician - he hasn't a musical bone in his body. Mylo has been accepted at UCLA – something to do with music. He hasn't my sons' flair, so I assume it's one of those non-degrees."

That was very depressing coming from Nancy who thought the sun shone out of them.

"Sit down. I'll fix coffee - or would you prefer a glass of wine?"

"Red please, large."

Once we were both settled I continued:

"Are you ready? Right. while Gil and I were in the middle of our separation, we committed an…" I struggled for a word, "indiscretion. It resulted in the birth of a daughter."

Nancy gasped and accidentally spilled wine down the leg of her trousers. I was blushing furiously so glad of the opportunity to disappear to the kitchen for a cloth. I slapped cold water on my face and fought for composure.

When I glided calmly back into the sitting room, it was to find Nancy had disappeared to her bedroom and changed into a clean pair of pants. She returned smiling brightly, which given the news she'd just received must have taken some effort.

"Why did you…hide her from me, and come to that, where?"

"I hid her because I didn't want us to do the same to her we'd done to Jacob and Mylo. I truly would have tried to be responsible this time round, but you know well Gil would only have done to her what he'd done to the boys. He'd have loved her until she loved him back totally. Then he'd have gone on tour and forgotten all about her."

I looked at her earnestly.

"You know he would, Nancy."

"He carries the world on his shoulders. Always has. But his priorities are often wrong. He should pray more."

"He does but it doesn't seem to do him a lot of good, so I made the decision to have her informally adopted. Oliver's mother Grace, who lived just south of Chicago found a family who took Christie in as their own. She knew nothing until she turned eighteen."

"What's my granddaughter's name," she asked avidly.

"I called her Anna Robson Maxwell. There were no clues there Gil could follow up. But her adoptive parents had her christened Anna Christina Heywood, their name. She's always called Christie. But I can do better than that."

I scrabbled about in my purse and eventually pulled out a dog-eared photograph taken when Christie was about fifteen.

"She looks just like you," Nancy said, peering at the scratched photo.

"It's just the hair and eyes, I think. She has Gil's nose and oval face."

Nancy was not a young woman anymore and had begun to look very strained by the shock, so I cut the conversation short.

"Can I get you something, Nancy? Glass of water, aspirin? Would you like to lie down?"

"No thanks Connie dear. But I would like to take a short walk just to sort things out in my mind."

"Christie has inherited that habit." I smiled, remembering her reaction at Windham when she fled to a nearby park.

Nancy left and reappeared a couple of hours later looking more relaxed and together.

In the meantime, Simm had arrived unannounced to pay a visit. I was always delighted to see him. He was a handsome guy but, even more than that, he was a warm and loving person. Christie was a lucky girl.

Even so, I didn't know how Nancy would react to him. Afterall, I was his father's partner as well as her son's ex-wife. What a tangled web!

Gil was the light of Nancy's life. Her favored son. It was to Simm's advantage his own father was pretty much at the bottom of his Christmas card list.

I should have realized Nancy would treat Simm as an extra son. I introduced them and she pulled him into her signature hug. Over her shoulder, I could see he looked surprised but pleased. He kissed her cheek in return.

It was just as well, as I hadn't yet broken to Nancy that he was engaged to Christie.

"There's another thing I have to tell you, Nancy. Simm, my stepson, is engaged to Christie, my daughter."

Both Simm and I awaited her reaction with bated breath. I hadn't thought of it before but there were going to be a lot of people to explain this to.

She looked confused and a bit worried. Oh hell – Monty, that should be interesting. I could sell tickets.

"They only met months ago so weren't aware of each other's existence until they were introduced by Grace, Simm's grandmother. I won't go into the relationship between Christie and Grace at the moment - it's quite complicated."

"Yes," said Nancy, simply. "When can I see my son?"

Chapter Fourteen

Death and Rebirth

Gil

Christie was out of bed before me. I'd already known she was an early riser, but it was only five o'clock which I would have thought was early, even for her.

She was standing at the cathedral room window, gazing at the silhouette of the mountain peaks against the opalescent flush of the pre-dawn sun. I walked up behind her and put my arm round her shoulders.

"You know, at the end of all this, that will be the final stroke of my redemption. No matter how hard we work, the mountains will lock it all in place."

We packed food and a flask of hot coffee each, ate eggs and bacon, put our bags in the SUV and set off for the stables, where we were to hire horses for the trip through the mountain pass. We were on the road by six, by which time the sun was striking sparks from the mountain tops.

I hadn't yet told her of our destination - there was no point. She wouldn't understand without seeing the place Harry, David and I had come across on one of our mountain rides from Anasazi. I was only praying she would have the same reaction I had, which had passed Harry and David by.

"So, where're we going?" She'd shown no curiosity to that point.

"Crestone," I replied, which of course meant nothing to her.

While the groom saddled our mounts, she tried to pump me for information. It was good to be in control for once. I enjoyed it by smiling knowingly and keeping my mouth shut. I could see her getting exasperated - she hated to be kept in the dark. She even went so far as to stamp her foot. My grin widened.

Once underway, we turned towards Anasazi. It was pleasant to enjoy a fresh new morning in the awakening Spring. Buds were breaking vivid green on the maples, and early flower shoots twisted their way towards the sun.

The crystal air was filled with bird song - what did the city have to offer me? I was always so stressed, so miserable there. Christie was right, I should never go back, never.

I watched her relax into the horse's gait, her thoughts a million miles away.

We rode through Anasazi with its sad, blackened ruins. I automatically tapped the pocket of my parka which held the piece of burnt wood Christie had wrapped in tissue and placed there.

The Snowline cabin had now lost one corner of its shingles. I wouldn't be able to use it again even if I wanted.

Christie reached across and patted my hand for comfort, just as the rocky ground began to climb. For a while we travelled side-by-side, moving to the sway of the horses and glorying in the towering peaks. The only sound was the clopping of hooves and jingle of harnesses.

But soon the mountain crevice narrowed, and Christie had to guide her mount behind mine as we moved forward. Sheer walls of rock rose almost vertically on either side, blocking the sun.

It was less than ten miles, but it seemed like a hundred before the ravine gradually opened out, and the warmth of the sun came flooding in, blinding us with its intensity.

Before us was the settlement I had known before. The same muddle of building designs of every faith and denomination under the sun. Tibetan, Indian, American, New Age, Christian and many more.

I felt my heart take off like a rocket as it had done last time.

The small cabin of light where I'd spoken to the monk Anukula still stood. We dismounted and led our horses across the central meeting place, past hippies, South American Indians in brilliantly colored attire, Indian gurus who gravely bowed to us in supplication.

Multi-toned wind-chimes tinkled from gilded hooks and candlelight could be glimpsed through the half-open door. For some reason, the pull of the crystal was infinitely stronger. I walked toward the portico, hoping to see Anukula but it was empty.

A small boy with a solemn expression and huge brown eyes bowed deeply to us and silently beckoned us to follow. At the door to a second smaller cabin we were met by an elderly lady who in a language unknown to us, motioned for the child to tether our horses.

She bowed low and ushered us inside where we were met by a young monk, shaven headed and linen robed like my mentor. He took me by the sleeve, being infinitely careful not to touch me. I took Christie's hand and followed him outside again.

I don't know how to explain what happened to me next. The nearest description I can think of was I suffered a seizure because I lost consciousness. Christie caught me as I fell.

Behind the cabin was a large open space which had been swept clean with infinite care, and in the center, laid out on a pyre, was my friend and teacher Anukula. His body was dressed in a clean linen robe, with garlands of flowers of every imaginable shade of blue and purple, pink and green wound round his wrists, and hung around his neck. The blooms spilled in profusion across the pyre and drifted, ankle-deep across the beaten earth floor.

My shoulders began to shake, and my eyes filled with tears.

We'd only met the once, but it was as if we'd known each other through eternity.

Christie dug me in the ribs with her elbow, which given the circumstances I thought was highly inappropriate. She dragged me back behind the corner of the cabin and hissed in my ear:

"Get a hold of yourself! Take another look."

There were several children of varying ages from perhaps four to twelve, laying prostrate on the ground at Anukula's feet. A lady in her thirties with a large wicker basket of blooms, scattered scented petals in the laps and over the bowed heads of a dozen or more adults - men and women, all dressed in linen robes, all with shaven heads.

Christie was glaring at me.

"You only met him once. Learn this lesson once and for all, and unless you want me ramming it down your selfish throat until one of us ends up like that...," she indicated Anukula's body, "you'll learn that no matter what your fans tell you, you are not the center of the fucking universe!"

She was white-lipped with rage and pulled me back into view.

The adults rose and scattered their petals over the body before filing silently away. The children, distraught, were pulled up by the lady I took to be Anukula's wife and the children's mother.

Then, something happened, which shattered me to the core.

Throughout the ceremony a young and very serious monk had been standing in one corner holding a large torch. When the whole entourage had withdrawn, he approached us solemnly and invited me to light the pyre.

"For your respect for our master and brother and as our guest, my lady has asked that you do us the honor of returning our friend to the Universe which bore him."

I looked at Christie in amazement and realized it was all she could do not to snort. I felt so ashamed. What happened next was either a message from Anukula or the crystal speaking through me – Anukula had said the crystal had claimed me – because without a conscious thought I looked, shamefaced at the young monk.

"Please ask your lady's permission to pass the torch to my daughter. She is truly the one worthy of respect."

The monk bowed low to each of us separately.

A few moments later, the lady reappeared from the cabin of light, nodded once, gave a small sad smile and withdrew.

The monk returned and this time offered the torch to Christie. He bowed. Christie returned the courtesy and took the torch.

She turned to me, luminous-eyed, and clasped my hand firmly.

"Come on, let's do this together."

I looked into the peaceful face of my friend of one day and a million light years, and a voice in my head whispered:

"Good - you have found your shadow. I can sleep."

He gave the softest of sighs as the air left his body for the last time.

I remembered my meeting with him, and how he had seen a woman's shadow ride with us out of the pass.

Still clasping my hand tightly, Christie thrust the torch into the pyre until it was properly alight, never once releasing my hand. As we gazed upon Anukula's serene face, she handed me the torch.

"He was and is still your friend. Say goodbye properly."

I felt the fire, hot on my face and shook my head.

"That wouldn't be right. The lady gave the honor to you."

She folded my fingers around the torch.

"Yes – and now I'm passing it to you."

Such loving kindness for the lost soul I still was.

I asked the young monk if we could visit the candle-lit cabin just once before we left. I wanted to ask Christie what she thought of it.

"The period of mourning is over," replied the young man, "My Lord has returned home - he is no longer here."

The wind-chimes seemed softer and more melodious than I remembered. There was no trace of anyone inside the cabin, but row upon row of candles stood sentinel, one or two newly extinguished, leaving a swirl of blue smoke curling upwards.

I felt the pull of the crystal immediately, but less overpowering than before. I was surprised to find I was smiling and the peace I felt was sublime. It would be the source of music for me from now on.

I supported Christie to the small stool before she fell. Her face was suffused with the same intense radiance as I imagined Harry and David had been so bewildered by. She turned her head slowly and looked at me in awe.

"How could you take fucking drugs after this?"

Oh Christie - to the point as ever!

The lady appeared as we left. She touched her forehead, took my hand and lovingly kissed the palm. She said:

"Not yet," as Anukula had said before. Then she repeated the same to Christie. I wondered what was 'not yet'. No-one had told me that.

Her smile was wide and loving, despite the tracks of tears on her face.

"Embrace your daughter. She also is claimed."

That was the first and last time she ever spoke to me.

She walked away and I hugged Christie so tightly she slapped me and pushed me away.

We revisited the pyre just once before leaving. My mentor had truly gone, the intense flames rose to the skies taking his spirit with them.

The same small boy who had led our horses away, returned and placed the reins in our hands, then walked into the cabin.

We rode off silently.

Chapter Fifteen

An Indiscretion

Giulia

We spent a pleasant day, Tom and I.

It was fun. No strings attached, with a handsome and attentive gentleman.

We tasted a selection of wines in a specialist bar. I had been dubious about the wine tasting because I'd once gone with Poppa, and it wasn't an altogether enjoyable experience. Pops, Uncle Peter and Uncle Sam all had a bit too much to drink and became embarrassing.

With Tom though, it was fascinating, and I got to learn the subtleties of aromas and enough of grape lore I wanted to read up on it for myself.

I trawled the antique and knickknack shops of San Clemente. It was seventh heaven for me, but Tom had no interest at all, so while I trailed round, he sat outside a café down the street and drank a beer. I came out with quite a few packages which he carried back to the car. Afterwards, we drove down tree-shaded roads to the Tennis Club and caught a glimpse of Bob Lutz practicing on one of the outer courts.

We arrived back at Ginsling House, laughing and perspiring from the day's pleasures, and I spread my packages over the table tiles to show him what I'd bought.

It didn't amount to much – a cowrie shell necklace and matching bracelet, a blouse with blue and white embroidery, a pair of Greek sandals I found at the bottom of a large wicker basket of odds and ends. There were other bits and pieces of junk I would probably throw away.

Tom laughed at the sandals.

"Why do you want someone's old sandals when you can buy Dior?"

"You have no romance in your soul. They may have trodden the sands of the Sahara or walked the streets of Kathmandu. They may even be the golden sandals of Hermes. Who knows?"

"Those had wings" he said laconically.

"Spoil sport," I took his hand playfully.

And that was how Simeon found us: perspiring still from our day out, laughing affectionately and holding hands.

I had a wonderful human being for a husband - I had cared for him since childhood, and when he was at his lowest point, I'd carried him until he could fend for himself.

Time and again, he slipped back. He was beyond my reach, alone in his own mind, fighting an unconquerable foe – most of which was his grief for Jamie - even after all this time. I could never predict his reactions. It was possible he might see Tom as a threat – or perhaps not.

And I? I was a helpless incompetent also fighting a battle I could never win. What harm in a few uncomplicated hours enjoying things I loved to do? Life was never meant to be so difficult.

I could see Simm was suspicious. Of course he was.

"Gotta go," Tom said looking at his watch, followed by the old saying. "Gee, is that the time?"

"I'll be back soon – just got to go to town for a couple of hours." said Simm in confusion. |It was the worst excuse ever, but I needed the time myself, so I didn't ask him to stay.

I had to speak to Gil. I didn't want unnecessary suspicions to cloud our time apart. Simm was Christie's fiancé. She was always going to believe his version of things and he would surely speak to her in the meantime. I didn't know at the moment just how I fitted into Gil's life – it was baffling.

I'd expected a call from Christie which never came, when they got back to 'Mon Repose', so had no idea where my husband and stepdaughter were. They were only supposed to be away overnight.

I was so impatient. I might not get the chance of an empty house again, so I made the call myself.

I was breaking her number one rule - no phone calls, no visits. But it'd been four months and it was getting beyond a joke.

"Christie, is Gil there? I tried to call yesterday but got no response."

"We got back late last night. He's in the garden, I think."

"Tell him its urgent. I need to see him."

It wasn't what you'd call urgent, except in my own mind. Although I hadn't actually done anything, I did wonder what might have happened if Simm hadn't walked in when he did."

"That sounds serious," said Giulia. "Anything I can help with?"

"No…no. Just some personal finances. I need his signature and it's important he gets back to me right away."

Gil rang back an hour later. I don't know what Christie told him, but he seemed thoroughly spooked. Unless you knew him well, you wouldn't have guessed. He had a very soft voice which he never raised.

"Hello Giulia. What's happened? Christie said there was some kind of financial problem. Are you okay?"

A flurry of questions. I started at the beginning.

"Not financial. I just said that so our conversation was private. I'm fine."

He put his hand over the receiver, but I could still hear parts of his muffled conversation with his daughter.

"LA…. problem, Is it okay……. you're…No." He came back on the line.

"It's a bit difficult, Giulia. I can't come to LA. In fact, I won't ever be coming to LA ever again. You'll either have to tell me on the phone or meet me at your apartment. If Christie comes with me, I can come to Denver. I'll have to leave the same day, though."

This was ridiculous. It was as if he was imprisoned, and Christie was his jailer. I didn't know how much longer I could be patient. I always knew he needed support but that had always been from me. How could the daughter he'd never known take over what should have been mine? I was beginning to rethink the wisdom of my care for her. I regretted that unkind thought immediately.

"Hold on. I'll be back in a minute," said Gil.

He'd gone to ask her permission. I was amazed he would do that.

"Okay. Christie will give us some privacy. She'll wait in the next room."

"Are you okay Gil? Why can't you do anything alone? For a man in his forties that seems a bit odd."

"This is not a conversation for the phone, Giulia," he said in a stern voice.

That sounded pure Christie – it also sounded as if she had taken over. Was she brain-washing him? I supposed you could call it that, but he seemed to think it a good idea.

"But Christie's your daughter and you've only known her five minutes. I'm your wife, for heaven's sake. Surely that must count for something."

"This is not for the phone, Giulia. You'll just have to wait. We'll meet you in Denver the day after tomorrow. That'll give you plenty of time to get a flight. Call me when you get there."

I managed to get a night flight, so arrived at the airport as dawn was breaking behind the concrete towers.

There is no place more depressing than an airport in the early morning. People are few, and most of the desks are closed. I drank a coffee from a dispenser, picked up my car and went home.

I slept fitfully for a few hours then did my early morning routine, which included the quick workout so astonishing to Gil. He always went off and cooked bacon, shaking his head.

The thought of breakfast wasn't appealing. I'd call Gil, and Christie I supposed first, then plan my day.

Christie picked up the phone and I wondered not for the first time if she didn't monitor his calls.

"Hello, Giulia. Okay if we're over about one o'clock?"

"Isn't Gil there?"

"No. He's built a shrine in one of the bedrooms – can you believe it? – and at present he's stocking it with candles." If I didn't know Gil, I'd think she was joking.

There was a muffled yell.

"He's dropped a box of Indian something or other on his foot. I'd better go. See you later – take care," and just like that she was gone.

I ate a whole tub of Ben and Jerry's.

I layered on the makeup and then dressed to kill in a silk blouse and yellow pants with a cinched waist -I even wore the dewdrop bracelet Gil had given me before we were married. I checked out my appearance in the floor-length mirror in my bedroom. Pretty good. Not having children had paid off. I had a great waistline.

Then I took it all off again and wiped my face clean. I looked sexy and that was the last impression I wanted to put across. I'd come to sort out Simm's mistaken impression. I shouldn't be attempting a Monroe look – Audrey Hepburn would be better.

I started again. Plenty of eyeliner and mascara. No shadow and a touch of lip gloss. I put on a pencil skirt, fitted blouse and kitten-heels and tied my hair up in a high ponytail. Much better. A quick squirt of Versace and I was good to go.

All this had taken an hour and a half, so it was now midday.

I made myself raspberry herbal tea and a tuna roll then ended up dropping mayonnaise down my blouse. I changed into another. These nerves were ridiculous and most likely had to do with seeing Gil again after over four months.

That was just plain ludicrous. He was my husband – how could he make me nervous? In my entire life he'd never done that. But then I'd always known what I was up against with Connie. There had been others occasionally, but they were one-night-stands and they had never worried me. He was a rock star and that's what they did.

But Christie was an unknown quantity. He'd never had contact with a daughter before and I could see why they'd struck up a friendship. She was feisty, strong and amusing. I was none of those things. I felt she'd overstepped the mark by walking in and commandeering him like this. I had a feeling there was something I was missing in their relationship. It wasn't natural.

93

I finished my tea, took a pill and calmed down. By the time they arrived I was back in control and feeling quite positive.

Chapter Sixteen

Giulia's Pointless Confession

Gil

Damn, I was nervous. I felt an ultimatum coming on and the one thing I hated above all things was confrontation. It was what after twenty-five years of conflict, had made me quit the band. I was just plain worn out trying to keep everything together.

I must have been fidgeting – I had a bad habit of picking at my nails when I was nervous - because Christie, who was driving kept glancing at me with concern.

"How the hell are we going to explain Crestone to her without mentioning the name?" I fretted. "The only other people I know who have been there, are Harry and David. I wonder if they ever mentioned it to anyone. Without Crestone, the whole thing must look pretty weird."

"Giulia seems to be agitated about something. It has to be that I seem to have kicked her out of your life. It's true. I have," Christie rolled her eyes. "Nothing…. absolutely nothing in my life has ever been straightforward."

"Damn, I wish you hadn't said that about excluding her. It hadn't occurred to me. Fucking self-obsessed again. I don't seem able to help it."

"Cut yourself some slack. You've been a bit distracted lately."

'I glanced at Christie. She must be worried. She was usually on my case about that one thing more than any other.

I gazed out of the window at the passing scenery for a few moments.

"Why am I so nervous, Christie? She's my wife. She has never ever made me nervous."

95

I picked away at my fingers.

"Probably because you haven't a clue what you might be walking into."

"I need a guitar," I brooded.

When we arrived at the Denver apartments, Giulia buzzed us up, without speaking into the intercom. I knocked tentatively on her eighth-floor door. Christie nudged me and whispered:

"You look nervous as hell. She can't eat you – she's not big enough."

She always knew exactly what to say to make me smile. When the door opened, I looked down on....

"Audrey Hepburn," whispered Christie out of the side of her mouth as Giulia turned to usher us inside.

"Come through."

Giulia was white as a sheet which only added to the Hepburn look. I glanced at Christie and sat on my hands. No finger-picking.

"I have….," Giulia and I said in unison, then, "No…you." Also together.

"Oh Lord," said Christie, "I'll sit in the kitchen. Which door?"

When we were alone, Giulia looked down at her hands, folded and still, in her lap.

"I have a confession to make" she said, "Well, not a confession – more of an explanation.

"Simm has a friend from school called Tom Beatty. He's a nice guy - you'd like him," she said almost pleadingly. "Simm has

96

been trying so hard to distract me since you've been away, and suggested Tom show me round San Clemente while he was seeing Connie."

"Nothing wrong with that," I said. Why the hell would she think this was urgent? "It was a good idea."

"We had a great day – antique shops, tennis. General stuff. When we got back, he had his arm round my shoulders, talking and laughing about the day, and I reached out and held his hand. That's what Simm walked in on and immediately drew the wrong conclusion."

"I'll put him right then. Is that all?" I said with relief.

"No not exactly. If Simm hadn't walked in, I know things would have been different. We both wanted it to go further," and she added in a whisper, meeting my eye for the first time. "I'm sorry, Gil. In a way Simm was right."

So nothing had actually happened. But it may well have done.

"Simm was so angry. I learned later that Tom had said he had a thing for me, although we'd only met a couple of times. That just made it worse in Simeon's eyes. I wanted to get to you before he did. You know Christie would have believed his explanation before mine. And she would have gone straight to you. I needed to explain first."

A stray tear ran down her cheek, taking mascara with it. I took her hand and held it in both of mine.

"If that's the worst I have to contend with in ten years of married life I have been a very lucky man. I know you suffer much worse from me. I want you to know from the bottom of my heart I would change things if I could."

I got up and walked to the window overlooking downtown Denver. What was this gorgeous little creature doing with me? How could I make amends? I had tried and tried to forget

Connie. I had deliberately stayed away from her for years at a time. But still she was always there.

A small hand wriggled its way into mine.

"I know you would - I do know. There's nothing I can do about it either. I have loved you all my life but Christie has entirely taken you over. You don't seem to have a father-daughter relationship. It seems much closer than that and I guess I'm jealous."

It was heartbreaking we made each other so unhappy when we both meant so well. And that had been the case long before Christie came along.

She pulled away and looked up at me.

"Are we okay?" she asked, tremulously.

"Yes. Of course we are."

I smiled, gave her a squeeze and brushed a kiss on her forehead.

"After all nothing happened, did it? Everyone has thoughts they're ashamed of. Its acting on them that causes problems."

I kissed her lovingly…once, twice, three times. I kissed away the tears from her cheeks and I wiped off the smudges left behind.

"We should ask Christie to come back in. She must be wondering what the hell was so urgent," laughed my wife.

"True. And anyway, we're only halfway through this chat. Wish I knew what the fuck I was going to say," I said glumly.

"Language!" admonished Christie, as she sailed through the door.

"My turn," I said to Giulia. There was an embarrassing silence while I searched for the right words. Christie tapped her foot. She seemed to be inferring this was my show and I should get the hell on with it.

"My problem is, I can't tell you the full story. That's because it's not my story to tell."

Christie jerked upright when I said that. I'd obviously struck a chord from somewhere in her past.

"Would you rather I left the room again?" she asked.

"No!" I said, panic-stricken.

This would be difficult enough with moral support. Without it, it would be practically impossible.

"You know that Christie and I have been working out a way to get me back on track." I glanced up, realizing how pathetically obvious that sounded so, defensively, I went on:

"Giulia, you know me well enough to know I can't do it on my own. Christie…well, you know what a pathetic waste of time I am."

That made everybody smile, even Giulia. I continued:

"We have been going through – one by one – the reason I am such a…." I was suddenly stuck for words.

"Oh, damn – really, Pa Robson? To paraphrase every half-wit sports coach in the country, there's 'no 'I' in 'be better'. And, by the way, the word you're struggling for is 'clutz'."

I turned to Giulia and shrugged.

"You think day after day of this is a walk in the park? I'm a fucking international superstar and she slaps me around all the time."

Christie raised an eyebrow.

"Well – fucking – stop behaving like a brat then I won't."

We must be making progress because at one time, that sentence would have sent me straight to the bottle. Now it just made me want to retaliate, which usually ended up in hysterical laughter because she could out-cuss me to a standstill.

"Back to the point, Pa," said Christie, serious suddenly. She turned to Giulia.

"I can imagine this all sounds like crap to you, but the theory is that he breaks contact with all people and things which have caused trouble.

"This is no mean feat; he has agreed never to set foot within fifty miles – well maybe thirty – of Los Angeles ever – in the whole of his life."

I could see by her expression that Giulia was starting to feel sorry for me. No. She absolutely must not. I'd been accused before of playing the sympathy card. We were long past that. The thought of the emotional fall-out from begging for understanding was unimaginable. I stood up and straightened my spine bravely.

"I'm doing okay. I no longer smoke or drink. The thought of taking any kind of abusable substance is too horrifying to contemplate." Christie pulled a face, "Until I can be trusted. It may take some time yet."

"Stop right there!" exclaimed my daughter. "Why don't the two of you take a weekend away? Pa, on my part, no more demands. Ball's in your court. You know how to manage this."

The thought was horrifying. Christie's regime was sure straightening me out, but my confidence was whacked. Giulia would be there. That'd be okay…. wouldn't it? I wasn't sure. If I got overawed, I could coerce Giulia into just about anything, whereas Christie was a brick wall.

"Go home," said Giulia. "We can speak tomorrow. Have a rest – both of you."

The fresh air was wonderful. In fact, so wonderful we drove all the way home with the hood down.

As we got into the car, I clapped my hands in elation, punching the air.

"And not one single mention of Crestone!"

Chapter Seventeen
Simm takes Nancy to Lunch

Simm

I didn't want to risk being interrogated by Nancy's husband as described by Connie, so I arranged to take her to lunch in LA. I booked into a little gastropub not far from her home.

While she had been curious about her newly discovered granddaughter, she was very concerned for Gil. He was still the center of her world even though she didn't see him often these days and hadn't since he'd moved out to Colorado with Giulia.

We settled in and ordered.

"I was quite shocked with Connie's news so I'm afraid I didn't take in some of what she said," began Nancy.

"I can imagine," I sympathized.

"And you and Christie are getting married? When?"

"I don't know. After she's sorted her father out, I suppose. She's a pretty determined lady - he's very lucky to know her. They cared for each other on sight."

"Its very kind and patient of you to support her – and Gil – through this. I can only thank you. My boys have had nightmare lives. Monty sacrificed them to fame and fortune when they were far too young. And all to satisfy his own ego.

"Until he got his first guitar, Gil wanted to be a minister at our local church, did you know that? He even went as far as spending evenings studying with the pastor. Isn't that just priceless? He never wanted the life he has, but couldn't bear to let his brother down."

It was plain to see that's what she'd rather have had for him.

I got the impression this poor woman had never got all this off her chest to anyone before, so I encouraged her to continue. Perhaps it helped that I was a relative stranger.

"Jamie was the worst. He was only eighteen and at odds with the world. He died of his excesses – it was a terrible waste. He was the kindest of people and great fun."

Everyone knew Jamie Robson's story. She didn't need to elaborate.

She had become tearful at her memories, so I reached across the table and gave her hand a squeeze. She pulled herself together with an effort and went on:

"Gil was just sixteen. He was straight as a die and so strong.

"Both of my sons were gifted. It was apparent other band members weren't in the same league. Jealousy is a dreadful thing – it taints the giver as well as the receiver.

"Ed, as the eldest, had thought the mantle of band leader would naturally fall to him when Jamie's addictions were no longer controllable."

Nancy's eyes filled with tears at her memories.

"He was devastated when along came this clever kid with such a talent for musical instruments and a voice sweet as honey. Gil had always been the kid everyone overlooked. He was just so young."

Her conversation was interrupted by the arrival of our meal. I filled Nancy's wine glass.

"My boys are a subject I can talk on for hours. As you will appreciate, we were very close."

She fell silent, then took a few mouthfuls of linguine before laying down her fork.

"I love to talk about them but quite understand if you've had enough. I would just like to explain a little more about Gil, if

103

you wouldn't mind."

I shook my head.

"I know he must seem to you a pain in the neck. He has interrupted your life so badly. Connie and Giulia will be able to fill you in on this part of his story better than I can. I was pretty much locked out of his life by this point."

She idly twiddled her cold linguine round her fork.

"You perhaps can't imagine the weight put on his shoulders. He was trying to control Ed, support Jamie, arrange all their performances, hiring and firing, trying to write his own music although he really had no time to spare, touring, arranging rehearsals and recording sessions….in fact, at twenty he was doing the job of six.

"Never, in all that time, did he receive one word of encouragement from anyone. No…. that's not true. Giulia, although we don't get along, never wavered, but he always thought of her as someone he needed to protect rather than the other way round. I tried to be supportive, but he was a grown man and a mother's influence wanes. His best chance was always Connie. He was besotted with her from the very beginning. This big-shot heartthrob would follow her around like a puppy. The feelings he has have only matured through the years. He can never replace her. He has never hidden it.

"Connie pretty much kept him together until he lost her to the sheer loneliness of her life. At twenty-three she was bringing up two babies on her own. Gil was away most of the time.

"After the divorce, the two people he loved most of all in the world – Jamie and Connie – were gone, and he had no-one, or so he thought. It was then he couldn't take it anymore.

"Jamie had introduced him to cocaine before his problems with Connie began, and taught him to deaden his worries with drink. But he was always in control of it where Jamie wasn't. He fell like a stone when Connie left. Giulia helped him by taking him out of Los Angeles. I didn't see much of him after that, but I did understand why she did it."

"Connie was my stepmother, but I knew nothing of all this. I was only a little boy, so the affairs of grown-ups went over my head," I told Nancy.

All I knew was this strange interloper, often looking like a vagrant, would turn up at our door, and afterwards, my Dad would shout at Connie and she would cry. Then Deborah would start, and things would go downhill from then on. The noise terrified me, and I would hide away in the pagoda in the garden. But, of course, I said nothing of this to Nancy.

That Nancy had opened her heart to me was a great honor and taught me things about my life I'd never known.

"My grandmother Grace found a soulmate in Connie. The three of us made a pretty tight unit." I told her. "Grannie couldn't bear to be near either Dad or Deborah.

"Instead of being judgmental, when Christie came along, she usurped Deborah's place in Grannie's heart. She helped Connie hide her from Gil by having her informally adopted. Connie was desperate she shouldn't be harmed as she felt her two sons had been, caught between a faithless mother and an absent father.

"Since Christie told me all this, I have often wondered if she wasn't particularly special to both of them, her conception the final thing they shared together."

Nancy's expression became stony, so I hurriedly added:

"That is absolutely no detriment to your grandsons. They were a case apart, and always knew they had you to rely on. Once Christie discovered she was adopted, she didn't understand how cherished she had been by her own blood until she met Gil. It made an indelible impression on both of them."

Nancy leaned back in her seat and I continued:

"She was brought up by wonderful adoptive parents who gave her a happy childhood. Throughout her teens, Giulia, with help from some trusted friends, kept a covert eye on her. Gil didn't know. He kept his word to stay away until she was old enough to make her own decisions."

"My son is an honorable man," said Nancy. "I want you to know how grateful I am to you for filling in these gaps. Do you think I will be able to see Gil any time soon?"

"I would imagine it won't be long. He's having a weekend away with Giulia next week. That's the first time Christie has let him out of her sight in months. I dare say Gil'll be glad to get away from her for a while. So far, she's made him give up smoking and drinking and of course, no drugs of any kind. He is forbidden from visiting LA for life."

She looked panic-stricken.

"Don't worry – Christie is thorough. She has worked you, Jacob and Mylo into the plan."

"Sounds quite a gal!" Nancy chuckled.

"Oh, believe me – she is! Connie, his friends and I are allowed nowhere near him until – in her words – he grows some backbone."

"I love her already," said Nancy. "She sounds precisely what he needs."

"Of course, staying out of LA means he has had to give up the band, but she has made arrangements for his music he seems to have found acceptable."

I spread my hands on the tabletop and shrugged.

"No idea what…"

"Now that will be something to see!" said Nancy. "Anyway, if

106

you'll excuse me, I have to go. I'm watching baseball with Monty this evening. Always such a pleasure," she said, through gritted teeth. "I was so glad to get to know you better."

I took a business card from my pocket and handed it to her.

"If you need anything at all just call me."

"Please let me know what's happening. And when I can see my son."

She sounded so pathetic, so as we stood, I reached and kissed her hand. She smiled and patted me on the cheek.

Chapter Eighteen

Giulia and Gil go to Maui

Christie

Pa and Giulia had a great time re-cementing their relationship on Maui. It was only a few days, but the sun, sea and sand were just what they needed.

I was surprised by Pa. I wouldn't have thought it'd be his thing, given that he was so laid back as to be virtually horizontal. I never knew a more indolent person in my whole life, except for his long mountain walks. All this diving in the sea and playing beach volleyball didn't go at all well with his penchant for steak sandwiches.

But Giulia loved it, which I supposed was the point. She was all Ambre Solaire and Gucci glasses.

She got a bit nervous on the way back. Apparently, Pa was eyeing the drinks trolley on the plane. Of all things, that was the most unlikely. A quick cigarette in the toilet would have been possible but having me meet him off the plane anything other than stone-cold sober, wouldn't have been an option. Even Pa at his worst wasn't that addicted to alcohol.

I knew it sounded as if I was some kind of dragon, but the various modes of discipline to get this job done were arrived at by mutual consent. It wouldn't have worked any other way. We both had to be equally single-minded. So far, it was paying off

The upshot of Giulia's nerves was that she handed him back over as if he had some kind of contagious disease. Then she kissed me on the cheek, hugged Gil from a distance and disappeared home to Denver.

So, step one of the regaining of independence for Gil Robson had been completed satisfactorily. We had a council of war over his glass of bourbon later that evening. He'd taken to drinking it with ice and water to spin it out.

He told me he'd only weakened once when Giulia, who had promised me faithfully not to smoke or drink while they were away, came back from the restroom smelling of cigarettes. He'd started to go down the route of 'well, if she can do it, so can I', but then he had the sense to stand back and take a look at the broader picture, which snapped him out of it again.

I was so pleased for him I danced him round the room to one of his own songs. I bet he was a pretty sight after a game of volleyball. Dancing to his own songs had not been an altogether good thing. For the most part, guitars are played standing still.

We walked in the mountains the following day. It was early summer and the alpine flowers were beginning to flush brilliant on the lower slopes. It made you understand why Julie Andrews did all that twirling in 'The Sound of Music'.

Pa was in the mood for singing so the heights fairly rang with his enthusiasm – bit like Julie Andrews really. I was so pleased for him. His mojo was definitely on its way back. I just had to keep it there until it was well and truly wedged firm. He wasn't stupid. He knew he had to work with me on this.

A day or two later, Harry and David turned up at the door sans girlfriends. It was really lovely to see them - after all, I'd semi-known Harry for nearly seven years – that's six before I'd known Pa.

Our good friends – ethereal Harry and David, chunkier with a mischievous smile that would melt glass – much like Pa.

Pa was out somewhere or other when they arrived. I now gave him space here in the mountains. The chance of him bumping into a dealer hawking coke on Riverside meadows was practically nil. He was always buzzing when he came home – but with the joy of living.

"Will you be staying?" I asked hopefully. Then another suspicious thought hit home.

"You haven't anything nasty on you, have you? If you have, go home now."

They shook their heads and David laughed out loud:

"Harry's known you from a distance all those years – he doesn't have a death wish. Gil's a braver man than me."

When Pa arrived home a couple of hours later there were hugs and backslapping all round and they settled down for a good gossip. These three could out-gossip any woman I ever met in my life.

The album they had all worked so hard on, apparently, was being looked at for revival but they weren't overly confident as yet. I loved the pair of them for that. They had stepped up to the plate on an occasion Pa had been at his lowest and helped him through his problems with the healing strength of music.

After half an hour or so, Pa kissed my forehead and the three of them disappeared into the music room he had constructed in the cottage at the end of the drive. I watched them walk away, laughing like schoolboys.

The following morning, I was awoken early by a crash so loud the whole house shook, followed by a thunderstorm without lightening. My room was at the side of the house so I couldn't see anything out of the window.

I threw open the door and dashed out in my robe to see if one of the mountains had suddenly become volcanic.

Davy and Harry grinned down at me. They had proudly just chopped down a huge pine with an electric saw and were evidently delighted it hadn't dropped on the house. Perhaps relieved might have been a better word.

A hundred yards away, a man in dirty overalls was knocking

hell out of the sedimentary rock of the hill behind the house with a pneumatic drill. A couple of his mates were making good progress too.

Pa was standing with his back to me and hadn't heard the slam of the door through the noise. David wafted a hand in my direction.

Pa turned, and I swear I had never seen him look so happy. Standing there in a pair of rubber boots and work trousers I'd never seen before; he was positively bursting with pride. There was a large cut seeping blood from his soft guitar-playing hands, and he was covered in grey dust from head to foot, that on his face black from sweat. He'd stood up the stretch his back and held a large spade in this left hand.

He jumped down a fissure cut in the rock by the drill, picked me up in his arms and swung me round and round until I was dizzy.

"We've started. We've started to build it. Just like in that new movie 'if you build it, they will come'!"

"What the fuck are you talking about, Pa? Who will come...where?"

"Our auditorium. We're converting the whole hillside into a theater for my music and my friends. Its months since we talked about it – perhaps you'd forgotten. And watch your language."

His exuberance was beginning to fail. That would never do, so even though I didn't remember, I hugged him back and yelled above the racket:

"YES, 'CAUSE! I'll fix breakfast." He gave me the thumbs up and went back to shoveling rock.

The exercise had made all three of my boys ravenously hungry. Once they smelled ham and coffee, they came running, barging each other out of the way to get to the food.

"Hey!" I yelled, banging a frying pan, not too hard, on the

111

counter. This isn't a scene from Seven Brides for Seven Brothers. Si'down before I turn the table over!"

They sat down obediently.

"Right," I said. "Hands!"

All three sat there and showed me how their hands were filthy, then sloped off to the sink, shamefaced.

We were all laughing by the end of lunch, despite aches, pains and one or two pulled muscles. Afterwards, we pushed the dirty pots aside and poured over the plans Pa had had drawn up.

It was really quite grand. Rather like a Roman amphitheater but smaller. They would cut seats into the rock in serried rows, and narrower smaller cuts to serve as stairs.

It would be some time before it properly took shape, but they were so excited about it I had no doubt of its completion.

The unholy din eventually brought out a neighbor or two. They stopped and watched speechless for a while. I fetched them coffee and one by one, they picked up shovels and pitched in to help. There was even an old latter-day mountain man Pa knew from his lonely hikes. He lived in a cabin a couple of miles behind our house, and wore a cap made from a dead fox with the head and legs still attached. It took me a while to notice, but then I wished I hadn't.

I was on non-stop coffee and hot soup duty. I got tired of making sandwiches, so I put hunks of bread and lumps of cheese on a board and they helped themselves.

At one point, as I was busy in the kitchen, I heard the outside door slam shut. Then silence. I went to look but could find nothing amiss – no-one come to steal the family silver.

Then in the cathedral room, I found Pa silently seated before the window gazing out at the distant peaks. He looked up briefly as I sat next to him. After a while he resumed his contemplation before sliding sideways and laying his head in my lap.

He lay perfectly still, and I knew this was a pivotal moment for him. This was the moment he became well again. This was the moment from which there would be no backsliding no matter what life threw at him.

When he sat up and looked at me again, his eyes were wet with unshed tears, but he was beaming with joy.

"Thank you, darling Christie. You have given me back my life."

He was prone to emotional overdrive, so I sat quietly and waited for the rest of it.

"It feels as if the whole world has come to help me fulfil my dream. I never knew such kindness existed."

I kissed his cheek and gave him a big hug.

"Better get out there and help then. Before they all escape."

The workmen packed up their equipment and sheathed it in tarpaulin against the night air, then left about four o'clock.

Pa, Harry and Davy could hardly move. Hard manual labor was not their thing, they confessed over stew and dumplings, which they were shoveling down.

Once they'd showered, I got out some antiseptic cream and dabbed it on knuckles and knees.

They lasted while I fixed them hot chocolate, but once that was drunk, they dragged themselves off wearily for what I bet was the best night's sleep they'd had in years. Pa was last out, dragging his feet, grey-blue eyes heavy with fatigue.

"See you bright and early Pa," I grinned. He grunted.

The following morning, I found Pa and a grubby workman examining some blue-prints over the dining-room table.

"Have a look at this, Christie," said Pa. "What do you think? If we chisel out here…" he pointed, "and here, we can get more tiers and construct a stage from concrete. It'll knock a slice off the cost, too."

"Looks good! Will you be putting some kind of wall up front? Otherwise, how will you control who comes and goes?"

"Good thought." He gazed at the plans and scratched his head. "Well, back to the drawing-board," he said to who I took to be the builders' foreman.

"Not really. If we narrow this bit here and make this more vertical, we can attach a wall across starting here," he pointed a broken nail, "and continuing across here." Gil nodded.

"Well, guys, I'll get on. How many am I cooking for this morning?"

Pa looked vague, so I went out and counted them myself. Five builders, Harry and David, Pa and the foreman and, presumably at some point, me. Ten. Oh, shit.

Pancakes, bread, bacon, sausage, scrambled eggs (three dozen), coffee.

I stood on the doorstep, banged a pan over the noise and nearly got killed in the rush. Damn, it *was* Seven Brides for Seven Brothers, but they did at least use cutlery, occasionally. Pa gave my waist a squeeze as I walked past ladling out eggs.

Slowly, over the weeks, the construction took shape. I estimated it would seat around two hundred – they'd carved practically the whole hillside away.

114

Chapter Nineteen

Devastation

Christie

Harry and David left after a couple of weeks for other commitments, but they were back, at different points as work progressed. Pa had invited them to play from time to time and I guess they were every bit as taken with the idea as he was. A meeting of minds with treasured friends.

Each time they left, they contacted the one or two ardent fans they knew personally by word of mouth. The absolute rule was that the secret should not be imparted to anyone in authority – no company men, no club officials. In short, none of the grey fence of 'experts' which separated them from the people who mattered to them most. Pa would have to work on his own friends eventually, but at present his time was consumed between his theater and his music.

On weekends, when the workmen mostly took a rest, Pa spent all his time in the cottage surrounded by candles and guitars, entirely obsessed with writing new material.

He was determined to do for his audiences what he had been unable to do with the band. Now Jamie was no longer there, he felt it fell to him to give them fresh, creative music. He was so absorbed I often carried away untouched, the trays of food I left on the doorstep.

Then came the day the phone rang. It was Connie.

"Get him down here. Nancy has had a heart attack and is at Cedars. Now! Or he may miss her."

She put down the phone.

The late autumn air was sharp, so I grabbed my coat and ran to

115

the cottage. He'd fallen asleep on the rug, his favorite acoustic propped against the electric piano behind him.

It brought me up short. How to tackle this?

I took his hand and gently shook him awake.

"Hello, Titch," he said and stretched. "What are you doing here? What's for breakfast? You don't usually bring it in."

It was at this point it began to dawn on him something might be wrong. He sat up, suddenly wide awake.

"What's happened," I was numb with fear. He shook me. "What's wrong?"

"It's your mother. She's had a heart attack – she's in Cedar-Sinai. She's still alive but Connie says its bad and you should get there as quickly as you can."

He was on his feet and out of the door before I could move. Most of the candles blew out when he'd slammed it behind him – only one or two stalwarts stood true and unmoved.

I walked up the drive behind him - we'd be doing nothing else but rush in the next few hours. Gil'd probably appreciate a few lone moments in any case.

When I arrived back at the house, I watched him for a few minutes silhouetted against the mountain back-drop in the cathedral room. I tip-toed over and stood a yard of two away. If I touched him, his self-control could snap.

He gradually became less tense and moved towards me, but I backed away. This was Pa's greatest test to date. I had to use the advantage, heartless as it seemed.

"You're not ready. Take ten deep breaths, count to twenty then walk the length of the room and back. Fight it. You're going to have to be strong - you will be needed. Anukula is testing you. Think only of your Mom and what she would want – no I in 'selfless' but a huge one in 'selfish'."

His eyes widened with surprise, and I saw him assimilate the thought, then do as I asked.

When he was back beside me again, I said:

"I will drive you to the airport. Connie will pick you up at the other end and take you to the hospital. Your mother needs you Pa, like never before. When you feel a panic coming on – and you will – breathe deeply and bring Anukula's face to mind.

"You are going to hate me for this, but you have to prepare yourself for the worst. No point in burying your head in the sand."

He raised his head and two terrified eyes bored into mine.

"You can do this Pa. All you need do is prove it to yourself. Now, take a minute or two to think, do you want me to come with you?

"I didn't know Grannie Nancy." That even made his lips twitch. "I may be in the way of people who loved her. I don't want to do that."

I watched as his brain began to connect again. I could see, although he was miserable, he was in control.

"Can I call you to come if necessary? I know I have to try to stand on my own feet. Dad's only thought will be for who'll sew his buttons and bake his cakes. Other than that, he'll spend his time abusing people.

"Connie will be there. I don't know about Giulia. She may come for me, but she and Mom didn't get on. Mom, who loved everyone, somehow never took to Giulia."

I was so relieved. That last little speech was all about other people without a single word of self-pity.

This was such an enormous 'ask'. I was trusting, at this time of appalling stress for him, he would stay off the liquor and not go searching for his old contacts. Had I been right assuming he had turned the corner when his face had been so full of joy that night?

"Go pack then call the airport. I'll sort Connie and Giulia after you've gone. I'll have to stop the building work for the time being so give me 24 hours."

I watched his thoughts flit across his face.

"If you say you couldn't have done it without me, it may well be the very last time you speak on this side of the great divide." I saw him glance automatically out of the window.

"Not that Great Divide, dummy! The big one. Now go pack."

"There's a flight at twelve-thirty. I'm booked," said Gil, a half hour later.

"Get in the car."

Gil called from the hospital. He'd been too late to kiss his adored mother goodbye and was in tears. I held my breath. What would he say next?

"Connie found her laid out on the bathroom floor. She'd hit her head on the sink as she fell. At first Connie thought she'd knocked herself out and shook her. But when she got no response, she tried CPR then called 911. They managed to get Mom to the hospital and linked to the machines, but she never regained consciousness. She's still on life-support but they're advising us to pull the plug."

He was doing great, although I could hear the deep breathing on the other end of the line.

"Giulia is here but not at the hospital – she's staying with her mother. I haven't seen her yet. Connie's trying to cope with her own grief. She loved my mother so much and was so grateful for what she'd done for the boys. She's lost her two best friends within a year – Mom and Grace. She's devastated."

That made the tears roll down my own cheeks.

"Where will you stay tonight?" I asked.

"Connie's asked me to stay with her, but I'll probably just go to Mom's. There's nobody there."

My heart bled for him - he sounded so forlorn.

It took every ounce of strength I possessed not to mention the demon drink and mind-fuddlers. But he really did have to prove to himself he could do it with no interference from me. I had to give him the option, so I said:

"Do you need me to come? Would it be right?"

"No. Don't come – not yet anyway. I'll get the funeral arrangements started, then Connie and Lizbeth can take over. I'm coming home for a few days."

And as an afterthought.

"Simm's here, by the way. He took Mom out to dinner a while back to talk about you….and him, mostly. You might call him. He and Mom had a friendship going and he seems more upset than her own husband. Not that that comes as any great surprise."

But I never asked the question in the back of my mind. Where was Giulia and what was she doing?

Chapter Twenty

Of Parties and Funerals

Gil

I did stay at Mom's that night. I slept in her bed. It still had her smell so I could pretend for a few precious hours she was still there. As soon as I got to her house, I flushed every drop of alcohol I could find down the toilet. No need to tempt fate. I wondered if Christie would applaud my action or give me a blasting for not making myself stick it out. But she'd said to give myself a break occasionally and I believed she would have understood.

Connie and I shared a few memories and tears together for old times. I was surprised I pulled myself together first, but I did. I excused myself for going home, but said I had business to wrap up that wouldn't wait and that I'd be back on the second to help finish the arrangements.

It wasn't exactly a lie. I wanted the searing cold, a walk round my building works and Christie's support before the service. But a new determination had been born in me and I knew this was more of a want than a need.

It was early evening when I arrived back at Mon Repose. The name made Christie double up with laughter every time I said it, so I supposed I'd have to change it.

I parked the car at the end of the drive. After all the fuss and panic of the past hours, the cottage was silent but not dark. I supposed it was Christie who had lit every candle in the place. It was alive with a flickering white light and deep shadows. My favorite guitar was still propped against the piano.

I picked it up and ran my thumb over the strings. Then the whole situation hit me like a train, and all I had been holding inside blasted out of me in a scream of grief. I sank to my knees on the

120

rug.

After some minutes I raised my head. The candles seemed to shine brighter, the flames steadier. My pain gradually faded into an overwhelming sense of peace. The more I stared, the more I thought of Crestone and its infinite tranquility. When all this was over, I would go back.

I picked up the guitar and softly played the most loving of my new compositions and thought of my Mom and her kindness. The song would belong to her alone forever. Then I blew out every candle repeating the same little prayer for her spirit with each one. The largest and brightest of all, I left burning.

When I pulled shut the door, I saw Christie sitting in the passenger seat of my car. Neither of us spoke on the way to the house. Neither of us spoke as I went to my room. I'd had enough for the day.

I had calls from both Giulia and Connie over the next forty-eight hours. They couldn't have been more different.

Giulia said she was still at her Mom's and would keep out of the way until after the funeral. She was aware, she said, she and Mom were usually at loggerheads. I rather suspected she also had in mind my absence at her own father's funeral.

She would see me at 'Mon Repose' if that was okay with Christie, on the tenth or eleventh. Her big sister Joanna was getting engaged – again - on the sixth and there was to be a big family party, so it wasn't worth coming, to go back again.

The Giordano's Los Angeles house would be turned upside-down by the arrangements she said, so she would appreciate Christie's help with the flowers for Mom's funeral. She'd give her the number of the florist they were using for Joanna's party. Not that I could have gone anyway, but it would have been nice to be asked.

It didn't seem to occur to Giulia that some respect for her mother-in-law might have been appropriate.

I was puzzled by her attitude. When I had been in trouble, she had pulled out all the stops to help me, even down to buying me the house in Colorado. As it turned out, I was a stupid idiot and reverted to type within months of our wedding, although it didn't last long.

She'd been a bit stand-offish for a while after that but seemed to pull round okay.

I was enormously grateful to her for taking care of Christie, and for considering her before my own selfish wants when she helped Connie keep her safe.

When she came to give her own little confession, I remembered her saying she was jealous of the instant connection between Christie and me. I didn't understand it myself so had no explanation.

I'd need to trust the spirit to pull me through. I'd subconsciously soaked up Anukula's aura like a sponge.

So, Christie organized the flowers for Mom. I hadn't seen them, of course, but I had no doubt at all they'd be spectacular. I later learned she'd added a modest bunch of pale violet and white freesias from herself. She'd bought them for their heavenly perfume she said.

Connie had gone to town on the funeral. She'd ordered the best of everything. She'd called everyone she could think of – she read out a long list – and asked if there was anyone else. I added one or two distant Lindreth cousins from Mom's side of the family, but she'd covered just about everyone else.

Connie's voice down the phone was so calming. She was her usual capable, organized self and I ached from missing her. The panic was coming back. I drew deep breaths and thought of my teacher.

I flew back to Colorado and walked the half-completed theater sitting on its seats for hours at a time, until Christie brought me hot chocolate and persuaded me indoors again.

My daughter and I talked. About music, Anasazi and Crestone, about Anukanu. When we were happy again, she promised me the mother of all jam sessions with her on piano.

We also discussed how to bring my friends to our theater and agreed that Harry and David should be involved in the planning.

Then I could avoid the journey to Los Angeles no longer. It was time to wish my mother a peaceful goodnight. This time Christie came with me. The 'no LA' rule had had to be abandoned for the time being and I was glad she was there.

No-one dressed in black, in stark contrast to Giulia's father's funeral, where everyone wore black from head to foot, and the ladies even had their faces covered in black veils.

Mom would have hated that. Middle-aged though I was, I was still in her heart, the little boy who batted baseballs through neighbors' windows and had skinned knees from falling off bikes. She never would have dressed me in black.

So, there we stood in our street clothes, in various states of distress, singing hymns we couldn't remember for a woman whose very life was a lesson in humility and love. For once, my voice was subdued - in case it cracked with grief.

I watched bereft, as the coffin was lost from sight behind a red velvet curtain.

Everyone but Connie, Christie and I had gone. With an almighty jolt I realized that the three of us were a family – mother, father and daughter.

My shock must have been apparent, but this time my usually perceptive daughter was way off the mark.

At the reception, as she helped someone to a glass of wine, she whispered "You're doing it again. There's no 'I' in 'Blue Moon of Kentucky – your turn."

I nearly choked on my soda. How the hell could she make me laugh out loud at my own mother's funeral?

"There's no 'I' in …." shit, she couldn't win this one…. The Brady Bunch. There's no 'I' in 'The Lone Ranger," joined in my cousin Charlie– "Or Tonto," hollered a voice from the crowd.

It was then my mother's funeral became more like Rowan and Martin's Laugh-In. I was glad. She'd rather we laughed than cried, as adults even. I silently tipped my root beer to her.

Chapter Twenty-one
Divergent Paths

Giulia

Joanna's party had been a great success. She arrived with Michael, her fiancé, wearing a fluorescent pink Lacroix which with her black hair, made her stand out in the crowd. She was slight. We'd both inherited that from our mother.

I was loath to go back to Denver. I had just recently realized how much I missed Los Angeles. Not the music industry side of it, which Gil hated himself, but its closeness to San Francisco and the best opera in the world, which took less than an hour on Momma's plane. I missed the Hollywood parties and the sheer fun of LA, too.

But when one was married to a major rock star, the kudos meant giving up some things. That had been fine. I had my apartment in Denver, which was no Los Angeles but at least had some night life.

I had friends there and supported a few charities. Gil never came to the fund raisers which puzzled me. He could have added so much money to my causes by singing one little song.

Gil's friends could be counted on the fingers of one hand, but they were lifetime friends. While they were good people to have around, I found their closeness a little cloying.

That apart, we managed quite well. We all loved him, so it wasn't hard to live with.

Until Christie. She was interesting in a very unique way - funny, kind and beautiful. I just wished she had looked a little less like Connie.

I had the help and support of some of Gil's best friends in my mission to take care of my step-daughter – including Connie's brother Bobby, which I found amazing. What kind of brother would choose his sister's ex-husband over his sister?

It also surprised me that David Ellis refused point blank to be involved. The best he would do is 'keep my mouth shut and, when it all blows up in your faces, plead ignorance'. Harry Forster only took part under sufferance.

I would have thought as life-long friends, they'd have wanted to do this for him. But David just said Christie had a right to a private life as she was growing up, and I should mind my own business.

So I wasn't very happy about going back to the mountains with their overwhelming sense of loneliness, even for Gil. While he loved it, my time in Los Angeles had made it seem oppressive.

Now Gil was getting his life back together, Christie had given him more latitude. Simm was visiting more often, and Christie seemed happier. Perhaps I should thank him for distracting her and giving my husband back to me.

That was unfair, I realized at once, when Christie was the one who'd helped him do the one thing which was impossible for me – to stand up to him.

In his own sphere, Gil was such a force of nature. Such a clever, clever man, confident in his own abilities. It was a pity the people he worked so hard for, mostly didn't care. He was just such a disaster with emotional attachment. He'd never been that way with me – I was too available, I guessed.

Thankfully, Joanna's wedding was only a month away and I'd be able to go back. I didn't know if Gil would want to go with me. After I'd skipped Nancy's funeral, I expected him to be pretty annoyed.

I hadn't considered any of this until recently. Perhaps it was

126

being away from him for almost a year; perhaps spending more time with Momma in Los Angeles or perhaps it was my brief indiscretion with Tom.

Gil, surprise surprise, was up in the mountains when I arrived. Christie took my bag, kissed my cheek and sat me down with homemade apple pie and coffee.

"I'm so glad to see you," she said. "Gil has missed you so much."

"Not enough it would seem to be here when I arrived," I countered. "I made sure to let him know. Which mountain is he on today? Or is it Riverside Meadows. There's too much snow for the peaks."

We both remembered at the same moment it was almost a year ago since that fateful snowball fight. Christie had nearly died of cold, and I'd truly understood for the first time how deep was their connection.

Christie had supplanted all of us – Connie, David, Harry, his other friends. It was most surprising his daughter had ousted his wife in his affections. It was indisputably true. No doubt at all, had Nancy still been alive, she would have been dispensed with too. But she wouldn't have minded, and I did.

He arrived in high spirits.

"Christie, you should have seen the mountains from the Meadow Pass. Jeez I wish I could paint. They…."

He'd hung his coat and removed his boots. Standing in the doorway in his stocking feet it was clear he'd forgotten I'd be coming home that day. He rushed to lift me from my chair and kiss me.

"Oh, I'm so glad to see you. A perfect day has just become…. perfecter. No that's not right. Anyway, how are you, my darling? I'm sorry not to have seen you at our goodbye to Mom, but I guess you were too busy."

He sang a quick snatch of one of his better-known songs with the word 'darling' in it, then kissed me again, beaming that smile which had always turned my legs to jelly.

The remark about Nancy, from anyone else I would have taken as sarcasm, but my husband was simply incapable of such an emotion. He meant it.

"Christie and I were beginning to get a bit concerned," I said, remarking on his late arrival.

That was a downright lie since Christie never got concerned about anything. If something was wrong, she fixed it. As she'd done with Gil, it seemed.

He looked better than I'd seen him in twenty years. He'd slimmed down and had more of a swagger about him. But the biggest change was in his expression. There wasn't a trace of the self-doubt or near panic I'd come to recognize as part of him. His eyes were wide, bright and purely blue. His hair, tousled from his hood, had more silver in it than I remembered but was strong and healthy. He fairly buzzed with energy.

"Giulia, I'm back to writing again – good stuff this time. That idea of yours about the cottage was perfect. I can sit down there for days at a time once I get on a roll, and that's been happening more and more. I'd like you to come and see what I've done to the place - you'll love it."

"Just out of interest, what happened to the hill at the back of the house?" I asked. "It looks smaller but it's covered in snow so I can't see it properly."

"That's the biggest surprise of all! I'll show you in the morning – not now."

He swallowed a slice of cold pie in two bites. Not everything had changed.

I was tired from the long journey and the surprise I'd found at the end of it, so I showered and watched TV in bed. Gil came in just as I was dropping off to sleep. He whistled – yes, whistled – and sang in the shower then cuddled up to me on the bed.

"Hey baby…pleased to see me?" He ran his hands across my back and pulled me to his chest. His medallion caught the light for a moment.

"Ouch!" I put my hand to my cheek and pushed away from him. "I got a shock from your chain!"

"Must be generating electricity. Perhaps we've a good thing going tonight," he whispered as he nibbled my ear.

Simm was there the following morning when we arrived downstairs.

He was neat and smart as usual, dressed casually in Jordache jeans and an Oxford shirt. He and Christie made something of an odd couple. She looked almost like a hippy in jeans and an embroidered Indian kaftan. Her hair, now way past her waist, was tied in a loose plait down her back. I had to admit she was stunning, and the look was all her own.

"I have one shit cool daughter," said Gil fondly.

"Language, Gil Robson," said his daughter in what was clearly a private joke.

I hated private jokes. They were rude in company and I could see Simm agreed with me, although he didn't look my way. The difference in upbringing became apparent.

Simm and I were privately educated and enjoyed fine art and literature. He liked jazz, I preferred classical or mellow blues.

If I had to study Canada in geography, Poppa got out the jet and took the whole family there, where we trawled museums and galleries and I wrote dissertations which put me at the top of the class.

Simm was a sportsman by nature. He was a pretty accomplished surfer by the time he was fifteen and had won yachting competitions. I looked at Christie. I wondered if she knew this about her fiancé – doubtful as no-one mentioned boats in front of Gil because of Jamie. She wasn't keen on the beach and was far more in tune with these darn mountains.

Christie was brought up in a family of academics, but she was an artist and musician by nature. When she played soft blues, her doe eyes took on a distant look and you could see she was lost in the music – just like Gil. I wasn't keen on the rock and roll though, although Gil loved it. I only heard her sing once and that gene she definitely hadn't inherited. By the time she finished, Gil was practically rolling on the carpet in hysterics.

And Gil? He had suffered all his life from his deprived childhood. He was a born genius with a penchant for live performance. And, of course, there was that euphoric voice which the whole world knew.

Occasionally, his past would manifest itself in irrational outbursts of misery or inferiority which were insupportable. It seemed at times he wouldn't be able to pull back from the edge.

When Christie came along, the whole dynamic of his world altered. It may have purely been because they were related by blood, but she spoke to him the way no-one else ever had. She bullied him. She shouted at him. And rather than finding it offensive, more often than not it made him laugh.

"C'mon and have something to eat. I can't wait to show you the place. It's so different - you'll love it."

He was like a little boy on Christmas morning.

"We'll start at the cottage and work our way up.

The roses I'd planted round the door all those years ago were still there. They grew right across the wall now but had had their winter pruning. They must be spectacular in the summer.

"There's lavender against the wall."

The scent must have clashed with the roses horribly, but I said nothing.

"What are these things here, Christie?" he asked calling her forward.

"Viola at the front and pink dianthus behind."

Ugh! More highly scented flowers.

The outside had been newly painted in a soft green and the roof re-tiled.

The inside had been redecorated too. One wall had been stripped to bare stone and the rest painted in a pleasing pale taupe which clashed with the door horribly. Around the walls were portraits, photographs of famous musicians Gil had played with over the years.

His electric piano stood in one corner and a rack for half a dozen guitars in another. They were full but for one - presumably the guitar propped against the piano. There was a plethora of scrawled-on pages spread across the floor and a jelly jar filled with pencils.

There were large, lined terracotta vases, no doubt loaded with horribly clashing perfumed flowers in the summer. Apart from that, the whole place was filled with dozens of wrought-iron candle sconces of various heights and sizes, all carrying the white church-type candles Gil loved. One of the big ones was still lit – an appalling fire hazard.

"It's for Mom. I relight it every day," he said sadly.

The kitchen had all the usual fitments but was rather old-fashioned with the exception of a large microwave, which was well-used.

The bedroom was Christie-inspired. It had a patchwork quilt and multi-colored embroidered curtains. Currently the bed was rumpled, and a used shirt thrown across the foot. Christie held up her hands in self-defense.

"All his own work. I don't come in here."

"I clean it and everything," said my husband proudly. "I come here to compose and when I'm pissed off about something. So I'm here quite a lot," he pulled at face at Christie who glared back.

"Your choice," she said.

"Harry comes here sometimes to play guitar. We hit off each other and he's better with lyrics."

I was proud he'd taken up my idea but there was none of me remaining. It was all Gil with touches here and there of his daughter.

"Come on, now," said Gil. "Time for the big reveal."

He positively skipped up the drive – very undignified for a portly man in his forties.

He led me to the hillside behind the house and began feeling his way through the snow and ripping up vast areas of tarpaulin. Christie helped him 'before he gave himself a heart attack at his age'.

I was aghast.

Where once there had been beautiful pine woodland, there was now an enormous ruin of crushed stone and wooden planking which had reduced the whole of the hillside to rubble.

"It isn't finished yet," he said, stating the obvious. "My theater will be a marvel when it's complete, and when we've demolished that bit over there."

Gil pointed to an area of cottonwood and huge rhododendrons, "we should have a big enough parking lot."

When I'd recovered from my shock, all I could manage was:

"Why? Why have you done this to our home?"

The boyish grin slipped from his face.

"Don't you like it? We love it, don't we Christie? And Harry and David have been up every week to help. The shelved bit we're cutting away there will be the seating, and there'll be a stage in the round against the back wall, and also a wall across the front so we can check who's coming and going. That was Christie's idea – she's practical like that."

The fact that Harry Forster and David Ellis had been allowed up here before I was, was not lost on me. I could feel my temperature rising.

By that point in his ravings, Christie had hauled him back to the house by the arm having read the situation correctly.

"Shut up!" she hissed, as I followed. "You're freaking her out. It's her home you're carving up. Have some tact."

He looked at her in surprise.

"I thought she'd like it - I thought it'd be a nice surprise. It's a place for music - it makes the house and grounds whole."

"Gil Robson, you are without doubt the stupidest, most insensitive man I ever met." I managed to catch this exchange. "Giulia isn't like you. Music is not the center of her universe. I would imagine almost the entire population of the world is the same."

"Well Harry and David understand it. Even you."

133

"Thanks!" she said, taking the latest gaff as an insult whereas, of course, it was simply the remark of an idiot.

It was my turn now.

"I know I have been kept away, but I would have thought you'd let me know before you cut down our forest and destroyed a large part of my garden. *My* garden, Gill. I planted and nurtured those flowers you are so thoughtlessly talking of rooting out."

I knew the expression on his face. It was rare to happen unless he'd been at the bottle. He frowned and looked defiant.

"I thought you would appreciate something that should make both of us happy. You're being deliberately awkward."

"Oops, Pa!" said Christie. She was actually laughing at him. "There's no "I" in thoughtful." His expression altered and he became shame-faced and stalked from the room. I was amazed.

"Not being self-centered is one of the things we've been working on, alongside the booze and white stuff. He just blew it. He hates it when he does that. He'll come round in an hour or two and apologize profusely. You'll see."

"I can't wait that long. Either I go in there and have a good old-fashioned row or I'm going home."

I was surprised to find I meant it. He was my husband of ten years and Christie had transformed him into someone I hardly recognized. I was jealous and hurt.

"No. I'm going home to Denver. Tell him to call me when he's ready to apologize."

Chapter Twenty-two

Rift

Gil

I was so angry I could hardly think. How could she be so insensitive? How could she be so plain *wrong*?

She had always supported and loved me. Now she seemed intent on taking back from me the most precious gift I had ever had. A gift she had given so selflessly.

I almost hated Christie for being right. I gritted my teeth as it came to me that that whole conversation was about what I wanted. At the same time, I could never take being separated from my music or my friends. Giulia knew me probably better than anyone else alive – how could she not understand what I was doing? This made me annoyed with her all over again.

When I left my room, the first thing I saw was my parka hanging on the wall. It was the coward's way out, but I left.

I started towards the mountains to think. Then I turned and looked down at the half-finished theater with its protective tarpaulins. She'd somehow sucked all the joy out of the enterprise. All that work, all that planning had been dampened in one brief exchange.

This time I felt Jamie again. He didn't speak to me. He was just there – I could feel him, his hand on my shoulder.

My temper died and common sense returned. I had to go back, apologize and try to straighten things out. I didn't know if I could give up building my dream, but I also didn't know if Giulia would compromise.

I stamped the snow from my boots and opened the door. Christie must have been looking out for me because she was standing against the hall wall with her arms crossed and an unreadable expression on her face.

"Go look at your surroundings and cool off," she said marching me to the cathedral room window then walking out of the room.

There stood the peaks, immutable, immortal. I shrank into myself as if they were sitting in judgement on me and had found me wanting.

The whole world knew I was lousy at confrontation, Giulia most of all. But I could apologize to everyone and it wouldn't change the fact that this theater would be completed and I would play there.

I began to pace before the windows, occasionally stopping to observe my serried ranks of judges across the valley. They gazed back blankly.

I didn't hear my daughter return but felt her hand on the same shoulder Jamie had held such a short while ago. The comfort I felt rushed through me in a torrent, but it carried with it such a wave of contrition and regret.

"Giulia left, I take it." I said to her.

"She sure did."

"Was I so wrong?"

What she thought of me had come to be my prime motivation. It had cleansed me in a way I wouldn't have thought possible, but I paid a price.

"No. You weren't wrong, but the minute you put yourself first your argument crumbled. Perhaps we'd better work on self-control. You were always so single-minded about straightening yourself out, I'd never considered it might be necessary."

Oh fuck! In that moment I had never needed a drink more.

"I'll call her when she gets home. I'll try and make things right."

"You know very well unless you back down or get her to give up, you can't. It has to be one thing or the other. It might be better to give it some thought before you call."

I promised I'd sleep on it but that was the last thing I did. I dressed and sat in my chair by the window, peering through the gloom at the garden below.

There was a brief break in the usually relentless cold. As if to echo my unease, the day had dawned with a blanket of fog obscuring the peaks. A damp melancholy dripped from each tree branch and blade of grass. It was a grey beginning with a dim diffusion of light where the sun should be.

I had an awful choice to make – my wife of ten years or my music and friends, the rest of my entire life in two words.

My thoughts, still whirring, were at least beginning to coalesce.

Christie put a hot cup of coffee in my hand and left. I didn't see her either arrive or go. I looked down at the steaming liquid absently, then put it on the table untouched.

I needed to walk this off. Not the heights this time. I'd go back to the abandoned theater.

I pulled back the tarpaulin I'd removed to show Giulia my pride and joy. In places, black was beginning to show through grey snow. It would freeze to ice later in the day when the sun burned through the murk. I lifted a corner and sat on the frozen stone beneath.

Giulia may not have been able to see it, but I knew the construction of this building intimately, and could see the beauty of it beginning to take shape even through its coverings.

We had all worked so hard in the planning, it was impossible I

could let it go. I'd have to see Giulia and try to explain what i
meant. It was inseparable from my healing - to lose it may mean
losing myself again.

I knew there would be consequences to my actions. No matter
how I tried, I couldn't kid myself that this was anything other
than my own dream, my own plan.

It was Giulia's birthday in ten days. I'd call her and arrange to
take her out for a meal. I'd take her a gift – she loved jewelry
and I was usually pretty good at finding something she'd like.
It would be soothing dining in soft candlelight. It would almost
be like courting her again.

Now I had a plan, I went back indoors and ate the breakfast my
daughter had fixed. Unusually for Christie she said not a word
but placed the food before me and disappeared.

I called Giulia's Denver number hourly for the rest of the
morning, but there was no reply. So I trudged down to the
cottage which had no phone. I'd walk back to the house later
and try calling again. I replaced Mom's candle first then lit half
of the rest. My guitar had stood unmoved for some time in the
cold room and was in bad need of tuning.

My half-finished composition lay scattered across the floor
where I'd left it. My eye was drawn to one particular verse, and
I picked up the sheet to examine it. It hadn't come right. I'd sat
for hours with those few bars and got nowhere. Now it came to
me.

I put a light to the fire laid in the hearth. It crackled into life
adding to the flicker of candles.

My fingers were numb with cold, so I blew on them and set to
tuning the guitar, humming the verse I'd restructured in my
head, so I didn't forget it.

After that, everything went so well. I straightened the cast-aside papers into some kind of order. The pencils, which had first dropped from my stiff fingers, sat easy in my hand. The notes and even some words flowed across the sheets, the music coming to mind at a speed I could hardly keep up with.

Finished! It was finished. I played it through from the beginning, adjusting a note here or there as I went along. There were one or two phrases I couldn't get my voice to, so I restructured them until they fit.

I suddenly realized I was hungry. The flickering fire was now a soft glow and some of the candles had gone out. Where had the time gone? It was almost dark.

Then I left at a run, only to return a few minutes later to damp down the fire, blow out the candles and stack the music.

Giulia – I'd completely forgotten her.

Chapter Twenty-three

Giulia, Gil and the Arbitrator

Christie

When he hadn't returned to the house by late afternoon, I walked down to the cottage and peeped through the window.

There sat Pa, cross-legged on the floor, head thrown back and eyes closed as his fingers picked at strings he didn't need to see. I couldn't hear through the glass but recognized the expression and knew walking in on him would be a mistake.

But this conversation with Giulia wouldn't wait. The only other option was to speak to her myself. It was an awful idea, but I couldn't see any alternative.

The man she had been married to for all those years, the man she had lifted from the gutter, had taken her ultimate gift and hacked it about – without asking her – until the parts of it she loved best had been reduced to a ruin. I could just imagine how it must appear to her. A phone call from me would only add fuel to the fire.

In her eyes I must be responsible for the whole mess. I had separated husband and wife for a whole year, and during that time his growing love for me, his newly discovered daughter, seemed to have wiped her entirely from his mind. It must only had made it worse that it was her consideration and Simm's which had made it possible in the first place.

I could never explain the countless nights he had spent walking the floor in an agony of mind, going days without eating because he just couldn't, sobbing into arms crossed on the kitchen table. The first few months had been a nightmare for us both, but painfully, slowly he had begun to pull round.

She had only seen the finished product. The Gil, laughing, joking and writing music again. The Gil she remembered from

140

her childhood, his eyes alight with love and laughter. The Gil able to cope alone with the deaths of his much-beloved mother and, at long last, his brother.

I sat in Giulia's sitting room and picked up the phone. Then I put down the receiver to try and get my thoughts into some kind of order.

He might walk through the door at any minute – in which case the bastard could do his own dirty work – or it might be this time tomorrow. Anybody's guess. I sighed and picked up the receiver.

No reply from the Denver number. After several tries, I leafed through their phone book and found Giulia's mother's number. She often stayed there – they were very close, even more so since Paul had died.

I hated the thought of this. I didn't know Carrie Giordano, but she had a reputation as something of a harridan.

So it was a relief when a maid answered the phone. In a thick French accent she asked who I was, and what I wanted, then went to fetch Giulia.

"Why are you calling? Where's Gil?"

Surely she knew the answer to that. I'd have known and I'd only been on the scene a year. I replied anyway:

"At the cottage. He's been there since you left."

"Incommunicado, then."

"Oh, more incommunicado than you can possibly imagine…probably. At present he seems to be on another planet."

She sighed and got off her high horse.

"I'm sorry Christie. I know you're stuck in the middle of something you can't do anything about. You may not be aware that this is a replay of what happened with Connie – two women crushed between Gil and a lifestyle he's unwilling or unable to give up. You can't even begin to understand the isolation."

No, I supposed not. So far, he was the opposite with me.

"Tell him to call me tomorrow. I'll be here until about two, then I have to take my niece to have retainers fitted. No. I can't believe it either."

Words failed me. Diminutive, style-icon Giulia Giordano Robson taking a child to the orthodontist.

I put the phone down, reflecting on the strangeness of life. At that precise moment Gil burst through the door.

"Giulia – I forgot to call her back."

"Already done. You've to call tomorrow before two."

He sat on the arm of the sofa looking winded.

"Shit, Christie, I can't go on with this. I'm messing with everyone's lives. I need to come to some decisions - Giulia has been patient enough. I can't see I've done much wrong as far as the theatre's concerned," I looked askance, "I've just done everything in the wrong order. My mom always said I was hopeless like that. At least I'm honest enough to admit I'd have done it all anyway."

"You just have to work out how to fit the rest of your life around your situation. Not only Giulia but Connie, Harry and David, your Dad and me." I said.

"You don't have to worry about Dad. He'd turn it into a three-ring circus. I'm telling him nothing. Harry and David are already deeply involved. What's Connie got to do with anything?"

"Stop playing the innocent with me, Pa. You know if Giulia was out of the picture, you'd both start up where you left off. You

142

can put a stop to that – if you do it from the get-go. I guess that would be worth a walk in the mountains."

He became more agitated than I'd seen him in months, and I was surprised to see his eyes fill with tears.

"I don't know if I could fight it again. It'd take more than I have to give to let her go a second time."

"Well, at least that answers your question about Giulia. You need to see her first though. You can't let her think you left her for Connie, no matter how true. That would be more hurtful than I think you could live with. Call tomorrow and arrange to meet her. You can't dump her over the phone."

There was a significant pause.

"Of course Connie might not want you after all this time. She might not want to fight you a second time either."

"You never let me down lightly, do you?"

"Why would I? This is your life. It's your job to sort it out. You're my Pa but don't forget Connie, who I've known all my life, is my mother and I love her too."

The following morning early, he disappeared into the foothills but was back within a couple of hours. He ate but didn't speak, then went to Giulia's sitting room and I heard him pick up the phone. This was one conversation I didn't want to hear.

I shut the half-open door and went to Gil's office to sort out a raise for the gardener who now worked exclusively for him.

When Gil came into the kitchen he looked shattered.

He'd called Giulia and arranged to take her to a supper-club in Denver as a birthday treat. No LA any more now Nancy was gone.

"What shall I buy her as a gift? Earrings?"

"Bit unimaginative. How about a couple of theater tickets? Opera? That's her music of choice, isn't it?"

He nodded and pulled a face. I took that to mean he wasn't big on large ladies with loud voices.

"You don't think she'll assume I'm taking her?"

"If the look on your face is anything to go by, I would think she'd probably know that wasn't your intention."

Chapter Twenty-four

Theatrical Explanation

Connie

The doorbell chimed and I answered it to Simm. He was composed as ever but I could easily see he was upset about something."

"Drink?" I asked. "Coffee or something stronger?"

"Large bourbon – neat. And bring the bottle."

Oh Lord, what had Christie done now.

I took the drink and bottle, as he'd asked, and sat down next to him. He took my hand and rested his head on my shoulder as he had so often as a child.

"I don't know what to do, Connie. Now Christie's loosened up I've stayed at 'Mon Repose' a couple of times. She doesn't seem to know I'm there. She wanders into the room, kisses me absently, then wanders out. Or worse, she kisses me passionately then leaves. We haven't had a decent conversation yet."

"Yes, Gil has that effect on everyone. Until all this is done and dusted, she won't have time for anything else. I'm not even sure if that'll be the case anyway. They have a very strange relationship on some level I don't understand. They seemed to click right away.

"I can't say I'm sorry about it. Its indisputably true she's saved his life. You have no idea what a miracle that is."

"Do you think I should give her up?"

The pain in his eyes was heartbreaking.

"The next move is theirs's if you still want her. In fact, the next move is theirs's in any case. Now Nancy's no longer here and

145

Giulia's between Denver and that damn house, Gil has no reason to come to Los Angeles. He seems to have completely divorced himself from the band too."

"Do you know about the row over the theater?" said Simm.

What theater?

"Behind the Riverside house there is a low hill. Gil, with help from Harry Forster and David Ellis, and with Christie's support, is carving a theater from the rock. A bit like a miniature Roman amphitheater. He intends using it as a private venue to sing to a few select fans. Harry and Davy'll give occasional solo shows too."

"Sounds great. What's the problem?"

"Giulia. She's taken exception to having her home and garden hacked about. Especially as he'd said nothing to her first. She walked out in a temper and went to LA to stay with her mother."

"Do you think it would help for me to have a word with her?"

He sat up and searched my face.

"Do you think it would do any good? You can see how I feel about what's been happening. We stupidly got engaged after a few weeks and I have to admit to a few one-nightstands over the past year but nothing serious. What must it be like for Giulia? She must be devastated."

"Yes, she must. But aside from their marriage, they've each had a certain amount of independence. Gil had his music – which to be fair, Giulia encouraged – and Giulia kept on her Denver apartment and her friends and commitments there. I doubt Gil was interested."

"So what do I do?"

"I can't think for you, Simm. Whatever you decide, I suggest you give them some space first. They'd only just met when all this began. I dare say they know each other a great deal better by now. She's put him through the mill - he might get sick of it all."

Absolutely not a cat in hell's chance. From what I knew of Gil it would drive him in the opposite direction. He was always so desperately grateful when someone showed him concern. I suspected this was his initial attraction to Giulia. She worked hard to drag him back from the dejection our divorce had thrown him into.

Monty Robson had a lot to answer for. He had two sons and he had systematically destroyed the self-confidence of each one in a manner guaranteed to do the most harm.

I suspected Christie was 'a chip off the ol' block'. In which case, Simm's hopes were dead in the water. Better to leave him to find that out slowly and hopefully less painfully.

These thoughts took place in a matter of seconds. Simm was looking at me hopefully, as he had when I was his only access to maternal affection.

"Give them time and space, Simm. Gil's getting slowly more independent. He won't need her so much when he gets back to normal. Meantime, he's got this project to keep him occupied, so Giulia will just have to suck it up if she wants to keep him."

He wasn't exactly comforted by my response, but I could see it gave him another perspective.

Simm had waited a whole year for her, but he didn't really know her that well. Perhaps their whole romance was an infatuation. But then you didn't wait a year for a crush.

It was a sad fact that Oliver's behavior had had much the same effect on Simm, as Monty's had on Gil. It was as if, for a split second, an icy hand had gripped my heart and squeezed it hard. I couldn't suppress a gasp. Simm didn't miss it and construed it correctly.

"All that was a pile of crap, wasn't it? You'll never stop loving him any more than Christie will. What the hell does he have the rest of humanity doesn't?"

I looked down, thinking. What was the answer to what was, at best, just a deep feeling? Well, I had to try.

"He's an innocent. His life has been shit, and it has eaten up his confidence. What makes him irresistible is that whatever curve ball life throws at him, he still loves – his father, Ed, his useless brother, the band. And me, although damned if I know why. All of us. You just want to help him. Unfortunately, for a woman that's devastatingly attractive."

"The very deepest cut was his loss of Jamie."

A sudden amazing thought struck me. Why had I never considered it before?

"Until Christie came along and filled his shoes."

His own deep thoughts made him miss my last remark.

"Giulia and I set this whole thing in motion. I just never expected it to take this long to resolve itself. If I'd known it would be the best part of a year, I might have kept my mouth shut. It's become like a chess game where all the pieces have been moved while my back was turned."

He paused for a moment then continued:

"I'm going down to San Clemente for a few days. I could do with time to think things through. If you see Giulia, and you think it would help, give her my number."

I had brought to adulthood a very kind man. I was so proud of him. What Christie was doing to him was criminal. But then, who was I to criticize – and how could she do other? I was just sorry my boy was so sad. It wasn't like him at all.

After Simm left, I filled a glass to the brim from the bottle and sat down to think.

I should go see Giulia, but I had a feeling that would have gone down like a lead brick. Even if I could have got past her Doberman of a mother. Perhaps I should call her? Same problem.

So I shelved that for the time being and sat down to consider my own position. I took a mouthful of the whisky, coughed and concentrated on where to start.

Christie first – less painful. Perhaps I could avoid the elephant in the room all together. No chance at all.

She came across her father at one of the frequent low spots in his life. He'd been bad, perhaps the worst I'd seen since our split. After we'd cleaned him up a bit, he insisted on taking Christie out alone for a meal. When they came back the click had already happened.

They could communicate without speaking and when speaking, she was allowed liberties he never would have accepted from anyone else.

Then came such a stupid, childish thing as a snowball fight, when they had pushed each other just a bit too far, and the fall-out was cataclysmic. The interesting thing though, was Christie had taken Gil on on his own turf, and arguably she'd won. At least he had come back to face the music which he never had before. It wasn't a bad thing he came off worse, but it was startling. He seemed to turn a corner after that.

But long before, at the meeting at Grace's house at Windham, I had encouraged her, in front of Giulia and with her agreement, to get to know him. I could never have imagined how completely that well-meaning suggestion would alter the course of events. But perhaps what happened would have happened anyway. Simm had no way of knowing the situation was in the making long before he came on the scene.

How did this fit with Christie and me? In my heart, she'd never stopped being my baby. Cathy and Julius had taken her away from me which broke my heart until I learned to live with it. I seemed to remember I cried a lot – but it was a long time ago.

Christie was exquisite and, from day one, full of joy and mischief. She was just.... perfection. Everyone she met loved her for her goodness and humor. The whole world brightened when she came into a room. Damn, she was so like her father it was terrifying.

I couldn't stop this. It had to be nurtured for both their sakes. Gil just had to – in Christie's expression – grow some backbone. Only he could sort this. Was he more scared of losing Giulia or Christie? That's what it boiled down to.

Chapter Twenty-five

The Prima Donna

Connie

I confess to avoiding thinking about Giulia but events forced it on me.

A few days later, Simm was with me for a short visit and answered a call. He handed me the phone without comment.

"You will please excuse my language throughout the conversation Connie, but what the hell is going on with our husband" – *really? surely a slip of the tongue* – "and your daughter."

"Damned if I know. What about you?"

"It was my birthday and, last night he took me to Young's for dinner. Best of everything, even a huge bunch of red roses…."

Suddenly she began to openly weep, great gut-wrenching sobs. For a few minutes she was completely incoherent. She could be a bit of a prima donna, but this was over the top even for Giulia.

The gist of the rest of the conversation was that Gil had turned up with roses and a couple of tickets for Tosca at the San Francisco Opera. Matter of sticking a pin in a schedule - lucky guess, I suspected.

Naturally she'd assumed he'd turned up to apologize. I couldn't think for what. It was she who'd insulted Gil's beloved mother by not turning up at her funeral - I'm surprised he hadn't hit her over the head with the bouquet.

Simm refilled my glass and Giulia continued her report:

"Once we'd sat down and ordered, and the wine had been served, he reached across the table, took my hand…," more loud sobs. I tapped my finger against my glass and took another slug.

151

I was losing interest in this tete a tete fast.

"….and told me he thought I'd be better off with someone who could make me happier than he could. The…. bastard! The complete bastard! How could he?"

I was getting sick of this same old line. So many years of it was just a little wearing. I was beginning to think Gil deserved a medal, though perhaps my next remark could have been delivered with a little more finesse.

"Why are you calling me, Giulia? I'd have thought I'd be the last person who could help you."

She slapped down the phone. She was good at that.

Simm looked askance at me and waited for me to explain. Of course, this was unnecessary since he'd heard every word of my side of the conversation, and I would imagine most of her's. She could probably have been heard on the Pier.

I gave him my best 'oh, really?' look and went into the kitchen to swill out my empty glass. I perhaps shouldn't have taken that last couple of mouthfuls since I had to steady myself on the arm of the sofa as I walked past. He followed close behind and leaned against the drainboard, arms folded.

"You have to cut her some slack," he said. "She may well be losing her husband to his daughter and ex-wife. Enough to panic a saint, I would have thought."

"Yes, well that particular saint has been in a state of panic for years."

I knew this was unfair and that Gil deserved whatever she could throw at him – literally and figuratively - under the circumstances. Me too, probably. That Christie had walked into a hornet's nest was hardly her fault – or Simm's, come to that.

"This has been going on as long as her marriage has. I'm just weary with it all. We have been divorced all this time and he just won't let go. He's made no secret of it. She can't claim to have been deceived," I fumed.

"Well, if you don't mind me saying so, Momma dearest, he's hardly the only one who could be accused of that particular sin."

Ouch! That hurt.

"I can't think what on earth you mean."

I sailed into the sitting room. Closely followed by my accurate stepson, damn him.

"Time for you to leave, boy. I've provided you with enough entertainment for one day."

He was immediately contrite.

"I'm sorry, Connie," he said, holding me by the shoulders and looking me square in the eye as if he was the adult and I the child. "Both of you have to face facts. It's not fair otherwise. Gil's at least been up front with Giulia. Don't you think it's time you got your act together too?"

I could feel hot tears begin to course down my face. Simm held me until I pulled myself together.

"By getting my act together you mean talking to Gil, don't you?"

He kissed my cheek sympathetically.

"I can't Simm…. I just can't. If I do, things will happen neither of us will want."

"You sure of that?" he asked on his way out of the door.

When he'd gone, I sat for a while and thought over what he'd said. Of course, he was right – he was always damn well right. The only person whose life Simm couldn't sort was his own, although he might get to it from the opposite direction by sorting Christie's.

I went to bed but didn't sleep. For some reason I kept seeing Jamie's face grinning at me. It was disconcerting when he was alive. Now it was downright spooky.

I stood at the window the following morning, The breeze was sharp enough to tip the wings of unsteady gulls and wrap old newspapers round the pier pilings.

All night long I'd had the same refrain buzzing in my brain. "I'd think about it tomorrow" – Damned if I wasn't starting to sound like Scarlet O'Hara after a bout with Rhett.

I'd think about it – if not tomorrow, certainly within the week.

Chapter Twenty-six

Invitations to a Theatre

Gil

The meeting with Giulia hadn't exactly gone as planned. She'd ended up hitting me with the flowers and throwing a glass of Chardonnay which some unfortunate waiter got in the face when I ducked.

But a little of the tension had eased, although I didn't exactly know why. Perhaps it was just that a long-overdue discussion had been finally broached.

Christie was non-committal. She could see everyone's point of view which was a drag but understandable. It made me nervous. She would take which ever point of view she thought was right regardless of who held it.

My first job when I got back was to corner Christie and set about renaming the house. We'd named it at a time when the title might have had some relevance. That had been in another lifetime. It was an age since it was peaceful – mostly thanks to Christie. The name needed something with a bit of spark, a bit of life, a bit of spirit to it. Spirit – I liked that.

'You can't call a house Spirit. What's gotten into you?" was her response.

'It doesn't have to be spirit, as such. A spiritual name. Is that better?"

"Marginally. Nothing to do with candles. Grace called her house Ginsling if that gives you inspiration."

"Weird name for a house," I said with distain.

was beginning to be able to answer her back. It felt really great, as if I'd accomplished something alone.

"Oh, Pa – put your brain into gear. Gin sling – not Ginsling. She

155

said it was because she couldn't get Slow Comfortable Screw Against the Wall on the plaque."

I nearly choked on my soda.

"You can't say that to your father, Christie. That's outrageous."

"I didn't say it. Grace did."

Neat side-step, I thought.

"We could just call it 'Crestone'."

I thought that was awful, just dreadful – a bit like calling it 'The Haven' or 'Mountain View' - or 'Mon Repose', for that matter.

"'Mon Repose' was French. Perhaps you should try another language."

In the end I settled on Jiwaku, which I thought had a nice ring to it. I kept the details to myself which drove her mad and gave me a great deal of pleasure.

After lunch, I wandered up to the theater and stood back to take it all in. We could start work on it again soon. There were just a few pockets of snow left and green was starting to show on the mountain meadows. Around my feet the first snowdrops were pushing through the chill earth, their flowers still small drops of purity on delicate stems. I felt for Giulia. I was going to have to dig up all their sisters to make my carpark. If I could have found anywhere else to put it I would.

I was paying with my spirit for my selfishness. Christie had taught me how to recognize the tension. If I could find a way to redress the balance, I must.

There was some frost damage to the autumn's work but mostly the tarpaulins had proved effective. I stripped them all away. It gave me such a feeling of liberation. The Spring was bringing a new world, and it included me and all those I loved in its exuberance.

156

For more years than I cared to count, my soul had been sunk in a despair I'd been unable to shake. My daughter had taught me how to grasp onto life. I was now able to pick up the skeins for myself and it was getting easier all the time.

It suddenly occurred to me that it had been a long time since the words 'cocaine', 'liquor' or 'suicide' had even entered my consciousness. And even longer since they had threatened to take me over. I looked around at the Spirit of Spring in its green and white softness. I would visit the cottage this evening and take Christie with me.

I'd been so lost in revery I didn't hear my friend arrive until his hand dropped on my shoulder.

"Which bit's next?" asked Harry.

"I thought we should finish the flooring first. What do you think of some kind of tessellation? Colored tiles? Perhaps stone shapes?"

"Bit ostentatious, wouldn't you say? Anyway, don't you think it would be better to start from the top and work your way down. Otherwise, the floor would get damaged."

The season was filling me with a new confidence. Today anything was possible. Tomorrow could take care of itself.

"I need to speak to you about invitations," said Harry. "David and I have it easier working from Los Angeles. We will need instruction from you for your folks."

"I thought Bobby could take care of it. He knows all the people who are at every show. He could pass the word along.

"Any more thoughts on how we keep this exclusive? All it'll take is one word in the wrong ear, and all the jerks we're trying to avoid will find us sooner or later. Then the whole deal is off.

We can't let that happen."

He was suddenly serious.

"So far, it's just word of mouth - we need to finalize what happens with invitations. Or would it be more fitting to call them tickets?" he said.

"Invitations – you don't sell tickets to friends. Is David planning a visit? We could do with his input. I've changed the name of the house, by the way. If there are one or two idiots snooping around that should hold them up for a while."

"Yeah, what's it called now?"

"Jiwaku."

"Shit, Gil. You don't do anything by halves. They'll never be able to pronounce it, never mind find it."

He let out a peel of laughter.

I rang David who said he'd hop the next plane and be here in the morning.

That evening, Harry and I strolled down to the cottage. It was so good to see him again. We made a great writing partnership. His style was more folksy whereas I loved rock and roll. If we struck the right note – pun intended – the two styles would come together like magic. Harry's lyrics were better than mine, but Christie was a poet.

She was also no slouch on piano, although she preferred the acoustic instrument in the cathedral room to the little digital one.

So, by the time we returned, Christie was into verse two of 'I'd Rather Go Blind'. Shame she couldn't sing like Etta James because her playing was immaculate. I'm not bragging, it's a well-known fact that I have perfect pitch, so just the sound of her wobbling off key every other note drove me insane. Harry gave himself hiccoughs trying not to laugh.

Over the months we'd been alone, I'd tried and tried to teach her to sing but it was just hopeless. I reckoned I'd paid my spiritual dues for the next twenty years. The oddest thing was, that if a piano key was almost imperceptibly off, she heard it instantly.

We had a wonderful evening, each doing what we did best. I even took Harry up into the pines to show him how the landscape's echo affected my voice.

David arrived the following morning. He looked as if he'd been run over by a train. If I swapped 'train' for 'plane', he said, I'd pretty much have it right. A couple of hours sleep and one of Christie's home-made pies and he was good to go.

We needed some kind of pass.

"Why don't you devise a code known only to the three of you - and me, of course."

They didn't like that – too open to abuse.

In the end we figured out who, of our combined acquaintance, hated the grey fence more than we did. We were surprised how many there were.

I had one other commitment before I could give my full attention to the outdoor work.

Simm had called Christie and told her he needed to see her urgently at San Clemente. He asked if I would be allowed to come too which infuriated me. She held me silent with a stare.

Harry and David agreed to stay on and organize resumption of the construction work. I only intended being gone a couple of days.

Chapter Twenty-seven
Revenge from Beyond the Grave

Simm

Eventually, I managed to summon up the courage to call Christie. I don't know why I was expecting the Apocalypse. She arrived at Ginsling House as cool as a cucumber and stunningly pretty.

Gil was with her and Connie had driven over separately. He was hardly recognizable as the same man we'd lugged down the gravel path from Jamie's grave.

The house must have appalling memories for Christie after her run in with Ed, but she'd never let it faze her.

I'd been named a Personal Representative to Grannie's Will. Instead of a year, it had taken nearly two to be published. Dad had contested every paragraph but it had all been a waste of time. He should have known his mother could tie him in knots legally. She had anticipated his every move and blocked it. But it had taken enough time to be annoying which was probably part of the intention.

Needless to say, he and Deborah were notable by their absence.

Everyone named was assembled, together with a couple of Grace's acquaintances and their children, round the dining room table to hear the reading by Grannie's legal guy. No surprises. It was exactly the same as the original Christie and I had already seen, including the small bequests. As expected, that left me as Rothschild and Dad as the Artful Dodger.

We all picked up our belongings and made for the door.

The lawyer, a rather slick character with brushed back hair and gold cufflinks, coughed loudly and asked us to resume our seats.

Apparently, Grannie had added a codicil to be read specifically at this meeting. Wouldn't she just? I thought it had gone through too smoothly. This was the bit she'd enjoyed most I expected.

"In the event of a marriage between my grandson, Simeon Maxwell and my adopted granddaughter, Anna Christina Heywood Maxwell Robson" – neat name swap which made Gil straighten with pride and Connie grin – "I leave to said Simeon Maxwell and Anna Christina Heywood Maxwell Robson my controlling shares in Westlake Recording Studios, and twenty percent share in Torville Production and Marketing Inc."

Gill, who'd had a cola to his lips, coughed and spilled it down his shirt.

"Oh shit on a shovel!" exclaimed my articulate fiancé, "Those are the companies Pa uses most."

Oh boy, I was loving this. The sneaky old bird had bought up shares deliberately affecting Gil!

The lawyer cleared his throat and continued,

"In the event no marriage should take place within two years, the afore-mentioned shares will revert to Mr. Gil Robson in their entirety."

This was the biggest and most effective revenge she could ever have taken on her son Oliver, my Dad. A large part of her business investments could have been made over to Connie's hated ex-husband - a man Grace had never met – but certainly to their illegitimate daughter, who Grace loved like a grandchild.

I did think this was a bit extreme but, hey, it was her money accrued over a lifetime. If she couldn't do what she wanted with it, what was the point?

I'd never seen a man faint before. There was a sudden bang and clatter as a small table crashed to the ground. Connie rushed over and fanned Gil with her purse. Everyone else, including me but excluding Christie who was laughing fit to burst, had run over to flutter uselessly in the background until some color returned to his cheeks.

"What the fuck...!" was all he could manage, as he struggled to sit up.

Christie brought him another bottle of coke and sat on a dining chair until the fuss died down.

"Don't fret, Pa, you only get it if Simm and I fall out," she chuckled.

It was at that very moment I first understood there had been a shift in our relationship. There seemed to be neither rhyme nor reason to the realization because she was smiling at me with the same affectionate humor which always stopped my heart. I smiled back, knowing for sure her soul was in the mountains of Colorado.

The lawyer called us to attention.

"That concludes the reading. There are copies for each of you to sign. I suggest you run them by your own legal representatives before returning them to Mr. Simeon Maxwell, Mrs. Grace Maxwell's Representative."

As Connie signed her name and handed the pen to Gil, I saw a flash of private sadness pass between them. It was so brief I didn't think anyone would notice, but Christie seemed to have a sixth sense where her mother and father were concerned – she saw.

We all went to celebrate at a new restaurant on the pier. The chatter of happy laughter complimented the mood. Lights twinkled on the ocean like stars, reflecting the velvet sky above.

I could only look at Christie, seated between Gil and Connie and wonder what she was feeling. She returned my look once

162

or twice and smiled, but never leaned to kiss me as she passed the table, as she would have done before. The ring still glimmered on her finger. Connie watched us closely.

Gil rose, tonic water in hand, and said:

"I'd like to propose a toast to a very unique lady, our benefactress, Grace Maxwell. I didn't have the good fortune to know her so perhaps I owe her the biggest debt of all," he said, very seriously.

"Thank you, Grace, for loving my child like a granddaughter before I even met her, and for caring for Connie when I couldn't."

Slip of the tongue? Perhaps not, but still Connie started. He continued without a pause, seemingly unaware of the effect his words had had.

"I'd also like to thank her for my friend and future son-in-law, Simeon."

He smiled and tipped his glass in my direction. I read nothing but sincerity in his expression. Connie gazed straight ahead, her face blank.

"To Grace," he said. Everyone stood and sipped their drinks then sat again. I remained on my feet.

"If no-one minds, there are a few things I'd like to add. Firstly, thank you for your kind words, Gil. Whatever happens in the future, you will always be my dear friend. Nothing will ever change that."

Connie and Christie were both looking down at the table before them. Christie was twiddling her fork. I continued:

"My grandmother was indeed a unique person, who dealt with the problems in her life in her own special way."

Grace's acquaintances looked knowingly at each other over their little ones' heads.

"Some people had difficulty with that. Christie and I have much to thank her for. She gave me love when I needed it most, and my girl was the light of her life for many years. She was mainstay to Connie when my Dad made her life insupportable."

I looked down at the table, unable for the moment to speak. I'd always felt I'd owed Connie more support than I'd been able to give. She'd always been there for me, especially when I was a child, so desperately in need of love and attention, and her own life was falling to pieces.

"Thank you for everything, Connie,"

I thought I'd said it under my breath, but she'd heard it and her eyes filled with tears.

We took the beach trail along San Clemente promenade strung out in twos and threes chatting and laughing. Connie and Gil walked together, smiling. I saw him subconsciously reach for her hand and she stepped away. My arm was round Christie's shoulders. I squeezed her to me and kissed her cheek. She gazed up at me with those velvet eyes and I was mesmerized. How could I ever walk away from her?

We stopped and I kissed her with feeling, and I saw Gil and Connie up ahead smile at each other and pause. I looked down and twisted the ring round and round her finger.

"It's over, isn't it?" I said quietly.

"Yes." She took off the ring and slipped it into my pocket. "It never really had chance to get started."

We walked quietly, hand-in-hand, back to Ginsling House. I picked up my car keys and drove back to Los Angeles.

Chapter Twenty-eight
A Melancholy Ending

Gil

I found Christie alone on the terrace gazing down on the strand we'd just walked along.

She sat on my knee as if she was five years old and buried her head in my shoulder. Connie came out and led her to one of the sofas. With unshed tears in her eyes Christie said:

"I'm sorry."

Connie made all the shushing noises mother's make in these situations.

"You can't live your life for other people, Honey. I know it's what Grace would have liked but she would have been the first to understand if it wasn't to be. You know that.

"Your father and I only want what's best – for both of you."

That cold hand clutched my heart again. How different things could have been. 'Your father and I' – Connie and me….me and Connie – and Christie, our daughter'.

I turned away, unseen by either of them and clenched my hands on the terrace rail. What a fucking mess we'd made of everything, Connie and me. It was a repeated refrain which just wouldn't go away and it was impossible – hopeless.

The following day, we drove Grace's friends and their children to the airport to catch their plane for Las Vegas. Connie drove back to Santa Monica and Christie and I flew home via Denver.

As we rounded the drive next to the house, Harry waved at us from the top of an enormous pile of rocks and shouted something I was too far away to hear. I noticed, with amazement, he was developing muscles.

Christie, who had been uncharacteristically quiet during the journey home, had disappeared into the house.

I waved briefly at Harry, then followed Christie inside. But she had already disappeared into her room and closed the door. I figured she needed some time alone so I didn't disturb her, and instead, pulled my parka from its hook and scrambled up to join Harry on the building site.

"Oh, man…are you going to love this!" mouthed Harry when I was halfway up the Everest of rubble. Davy, red-faced and sweating, appeared behind him. He was beaming ear to ear. The cacophony was appalling.

On top of the mound was a rickety trestle table with one leg propped up on a piece of stone to hold it level. Stretched across it were the plans we'd drawn up before I'd left, trying to whip free from the rocks holding them in place in a stiff breeze.

Below must have been thirty workmen with diggers, drills, picks, mechanical shovels and every other possible instrument of construction – or in this case, destruction – known to man.

"Oh my fuckin' God, Harry," I yelled. "Where did you get them from?"

Davy was practically jumping up and down with glee.

"Giulia sent them."

"She did WHAT!" I hollered. David nodded,

"She said if you were going to ditch her, she'd make sure you did a proper job. She said you could have your fucking theater – her words - and she hoped you'd bury yourself up to your fucking neck in it – also her words. She sent Godzilla and his cohorts to make sure."

My legs gave way and I sat down hard on a nearby rock, unable to shut my mouth.

David, still jumping up and down said:

166

"Told you he'd like it! Told you! Now all he has to do is sort Giulia out. Easy!"

I tried with difficulty, to ignore them. Laid out before me were the bare bones of the completed theater. One of the diggers was in the process of tipping excess stone blocks down the side of the building and they were being faced with soil ready for grassing. Tier upon tier of rough stone steps, about two foot tall and three feet deep, ended in a circular area maybe forty yards in diameter against the back wall.

"Tell Godzilla and his cohorts to take ten – or better still, give them the rest of the day off," I said to David, and began clambering down. To hell with Christie's finer feelings – she was going to see this now.

I ran in the house and banged on her door with my fist.

"Christie – I need you out here – NOW!"

"Go away," said a muffled voice.

'NO…NOW!"

She told me later she thought she'd opened the door to a hobo. My jeans were ripped at the knee and showed bloody grazes beneath. There was a gash on my forehead, and I was covered in dust from head to foot. It was only half an hour since she'd left me.

I grabbed her hand, dragged her out of the house and began physically hauling her to the top of the stones. By the time we got there she was spitting fire.

"Get your goddam hands off me, you son-of-a-bitch. Fuck off!"

I grabbed her by the shoulders and turned her round a hundred and eighty degrees. She fell back against me in shock.

"What the…..."

"My thoughts exactly," I managed to choke out. "Giulia sent them – she sent them. Oh jeez."

There's an expression 'It was enough to make a grown man cry'. How accurate it was.

Christie was suddenly serious.

"You have to go see her. I want to know why. Nobody's that generous without a reason."

Once ensconced in the warm kitchen, and before Harry and David could join us, I said:

"Giulia hates what I've done, she hates that it has taken over my life because she doesn't understand it, She hates that the whole world has revolved and not taken her with it. But me she loves. There is nothing to be done about it, any more than there is for Connie and I. Life can be a bitch."

"Only one thing wrong with that statement, you pompous ass Giulia loves you – indisputably – and you love Connie, also indisputable. But – dumbass – the difference is, Connie loves you back. Or are you both so lacking in brains you can't see what's staring you in the face!"

I could feel my temperature start to rise. I'd indulged her too much.

Harry and Davy chose that moment to walk in, laughing and chattering. I glared an instruction for silence at Christie and stood up.

"Hi guys! I think I've spread enough muck around this part of the house," Christie raised a scornful eyebrow, "so going to get showered. Suggest you do the same before this one rips the clothes off your backs and sticks them in the laundry unasked.

My spitfire took a step forward as if to do just that and they were gone. She stood and folded her arms.

"We're not done yet," she scowled.

I followed them out, pronto.

I slept uneasily that night and when I'd been tossing and turning for an hour, I got up and wandered to the silent theatre, sitting on the retaining wall above the seating. The mountains were bathed in the light of a full moon – mystical, enticing. I took a deep breath of the cleansing air.

As I stood gazing upon the miracle of the mountains, the theater seemed to wake and called to me as if music was already alive in its stones. It beckoned. If I would only step nearer, I would hear it.

I stumbled over the rough ground to the gateway. They had begun to lay the floor in ochre and terracotta colored stone. Still I couldn't hear, only feel, the melodies.

"It's waiting for you to make the songs," said a man's voice behind me. I turned but only saw Christie materialize out of the shadows.

"I heard him too," she said. "He's right."

We spent the rest of the night in the cottage. I played and wrote more easily – and better - than I had in my entire life. Christie sat by the fire, or walked softly round the room, replenishing burnt-out candles, then idly making up wonderful poetry for my melodies.

Until I supplied its songs, the stage was dead, empty stone. It had no purpose, no life. It needed to be alight with laughter, and with music to touch the very stars. It needed all my friends, Harry and David too.

As we walked back up the drive, I said to Christie:

"I have to go to Crestone tomorrow. Alone. I'll get a little sleep first. Can you pack me some food?"

For the first time in years, I felt needed in a way I had never experienced since childhood at my mother's knee. It was intoxicating but I needed prayer to do what I had to do, and Crestone was the best, the only place to go.

"I'll need you and the guys to keep the work on track. Will you do that?"

Christie woke me early, gave me breakfast and the food she'd packed.

"I've called the stables. They've a horse waiting for you."

"Thank you for this, Christie. Thank you for not trying to talk sense into me."

I spent that night in the candle-lit cabin with the soft tinkle of wind-chimes for company. The lady was there, but she hurried her playing children away when she saw me ride up.

The peace was intoxicating. The warmth from the crystal flooded me entirely. Answers to the prayers I sent out were whispered back to me, soft as the chimes outside.

By morning, I felt I could have flown home. My body was as light as air and my soul with it.

I found bread, soft cheese and potato cakes, on the cabin porch. One or two people were stirring but I saw nothing of Anukula's family. There were only a few children playing in the dust outside the Catholic church, and brightly clad women drew water from a well.

The coin I left on my empty plate would mean nothing to them, except food to fill the children's bellies. They would know it wasn't meant as payment. What they gave was free.

When I got back, I called a council of war. I felt so invigorated I fetched pencil and paper and wrote:

'Jobs to do'

Harry and David slid onto the benches next to the table. Harry had a creased forehead and looked a bit worried.

"Before we start, we need to decide whether we're doing solo shows, or do we do a combination?"

It was a long, long afternoon. In the old days I'd have sunk at least a bottle of JD over it. Now, of course, it was soda and coffee which was definitely more productive.

We concluded that the first show should be mine, then we'd talk who did what show by show. Now we didn't have bands and support acts to lug about we could do pretty much as we pleased. None of us were exactly on the breadline so we decided to scrap any entrance fees. And I owned the venue – that was such a buzz.

While Christie appreciated the raw beauty of the place, she did suggest we got a stone mason in to provide a little finesse. I couldn't decide if there was sarcasm in her remark or she was just being herself... perhaps the difference was marginal. Whatever the case, that became her job.

We'd got most of it sorted but this 'secrecy' thing was impossible.

While we were scratching our heads and were thoroughly distracted, we didn't notice the construction foreman was standing in the hall.

He quietly excused himself for the interruption and said:

"You guys considered there might be workers amongst your people in the audience? It's just that you seem to trust them."

"Yeah, true," said David. but what about all your guys? There must be over thirty of them."

"I don't think they'll be a problem. Between job losses and free entry to your shows, I think they'll pretty much toe the line."

"We've decided no children. With the best will in the world you can't stop a ten-year-old from sharing secrets," said Harry who had a ten-year-old. "Would they go for that?"

"Oh, I would think that'd be a plus point," grinned the foreman.

When he'd left and we'd been mulling it over for a while, I noticed that Christie was quiet and lost in thought. Eventually she said:

"You know, we could always use a bit of psychology. Why don't we use them as security? Might make them feel part of the whole secrecy thing. Kids can't keep secrets, Harry, but adults can if they feel they're amongst the favored few. Even better, we have an expert on hand – Maurice!"

Frankly, I had difficulty remembering what he looked like. He'd had the charge of Ginsling House for a long time now so perhaps would appreciate being remembered.

"It's far from perfect," I said. "But I think it's the best we can do for now. You call Maurice."

I could see there were holes in this plan as big as the Pico Tunnel. I'd just have to light more candles and pray harder. By the look on the others' faces, they might be joining me.

At least we now had a working plan. We gave ourselves a time schedule of three months which would get us well into the summer. Then we could start putting out the word.

Next, I had to tackle that goddamn parking lot. Which brought on another unwelcome thought. I couldn't in all conscience put off visiting Giulia any longer.

Chapter Twenty-nine

A Slap in the Face for Giulia

Giulia

As luck would have it, Tom was visiting from Los Angeles when Gil knocked on the door.

The apartment block I owned could only be accessed by release from inside. But Gil had slipped through behind one of the residents, so I didn't hear him until he rapped at the door.

I introduced Tom. Gil knew who he was as soon as I mentioned his name. I felt a bit hurt to see my husband of years didn't even flinch but put out his hand for Tom to shake. Tom, however looked decidedly nervous.

"I'll call you, Giulia," he said, never taking his eyes from Gil.

Gil acknowledged his courtesy with a smile.

My God! It was like a reunion of long lost friends!

I closed the door when Tom left and returned to my sitting room ready to do battle.

I should have known better. I had only seen Gil riled to the point of fury once in the whole of our lives together. That was when I refused to tell him where Christie was. Usually, he tried to see the other person's point of view. Infuriatingly, this was one of those times.

"I've come to try to put things right between us Giulia. It's clear we have to part ways, but I would like for us to do it on good terms if at all possible."

I stared at him, completely speechless, then burst into tears. He wouldn't know it, but they were as much of fury as distress. I had given him my whole self - body, heart and soul, the second two for a lifetime.

I had given him the home he was now hacking to pieces with

174

the help of that goddamn daughter of his. It was infuriating. I loved her probably as much as I would my own child. That made me even more irate and more tearful.

He hugged me for comfort. It was a relief to slap his face.

"I don't know what to say to you Gil," - I'd go for the jugular here - "How can I ever recover from this? I'm past thirty. My best years are gone. I gave them all to you."

He sat on the edge of the sofa and turned his head away from me in shame.

"Tell me what I can do to make things right," he muttered. Right!

"Well, to begin with, you can give me back the gift I gave you with so much love. I want the house – all of it."

That got his attention. His head snapped round and he stared at me.

"You know I can't do that. You talk about heart and soul. My whole being is invested in that theater. You are welcome to the house if you want it. I'll figure something out. But I can't let the theater go."

That was like a slap in the face. He could give back the house I'd gifted because I loved him so much. Yet he wanted to keep the grounds? He wanted to desecrate my garden and let me live in the house, watching all kinds of strangers drive through it and park in the area where my bulbs had been so lovingly planted?

"No. All of it."

All my actions depended on anticipating his response. I didn't expect what he did next.

He picked up a priceless Wedgewood vase my mother had given me and flung it across the room at the windows. We were eight stories up so it was fortunate they didn't crack, but the vase was destroyed beyond repair.

I dashed to pick up the pieces, but he was there before me, trying uselessly to fit them back together, devastated by his lack of control.

"Sorry, Giulia. I am so sorry. Please forgive me. I'm so sorry."

"Get out of my home you son-of-a-bitch. If you ever come back, you'll do time. Do you understand me? Now go to hell."

He looked shocked and left at the double.

Tom had sat in his car and waited for Gil to leave, before rapping at my door again and asking if I was alright.

I sobbed into his chest, my fingers clenched in his shirt, then looked up at him still gasping.

"I gave him all I had for as long as I can remember. But he never, ever lied to me. Not once. I always knew I was second best. Connie I have known even longer. Those he loves, I do too."

I must have looked dreadful, mascara streaked down my face, my lipstick smudged.

"Divorce him?" Tom replied as he walked to the phone.

"What are you doing?"

"Calling Simm. Christie might have more idea what's going on."

After several minutes' conversation, he put down the receiver and looked up at me pensively.

"They've split up too. He doesn't know why - she just seemed to switch off. He's spoken to Connie – she's just as confused as we are."

I didn't believe that for one second. Connie always knew what Gil was thinking – always had.

"They're both consumed by thoughts of this theater. Simm

claims the original idea for his, but I'd lay money on it coming from Christie when she was helping him get over his addictions. It just took off. Neither of them seemed capable of thinking about anything else. They've dragged Harry Forster and David Ellis into it as well," Tom said.

"They won't have needed much dragging," I said ironically. "They're the three musical musketeers."

The mental imagery made us grin, despite the situation.

"You have such a beautiful smile. You should use it more often," Tom said passionately.

But the conversation gave me a clue as to what I should do next.

If, as I suspected, Connie knew more than she was letting on, I'd get it out of her one way or another. She didn't scare me, I thought without conviction.

I kissed Tom goodbye, packed a few necessary items and headed for home, my Momma's house in LA. I only intended an overnight stay. I didn't want her wading into Connie before I'd had time to get what I wanted. I'd drop off my stuff and take the half hour drive to Santa Monica.

When I arrived at Connie's, Simm's car was parked in the 'port. I nearly turned right round and left. But Simm was the one person on earth who might understand my situation, so I climbed the steps and rang the bell.

It was clear they were expecting me. Simm must have anticipated Connie would be my first call. She stood aside to let me in.

Simm gave me a sympathetic hug and ended up with cherry-red lipstick on his shirt.

"You've come to ask me what Gil's doing?" asked Connie. "Sorry, I haven't a freakin' clue. I'd like to know myself and I intend finding out. Do we draw lots for who goes?"

"Or we could send Simm," I said, ironically.

He looked away and shook his head repeatedly. Connie sat on his chair arm and ran her fingers through his hair.

"Well, you could have tried a little tact," she glared.

"Oh, I'm long past tact," I said. "The bastard smashed a priceless Wedgewood vase in temper. He'll pay for that….and I don't mean the vase. Well, that too.

"I am assuming he's ditched ten years of marriage for a ruined hillside, but I need to know for certain. Then I'll decide what to do next because no way am I going back to living in that house. I gave him the deeds as a gift but if he's downright determined to keep the house, I'll make him pay."

"I don't think you'll have a problem with the money. He'll put it in an envelope and give it to you if he ends up with the house and grounds. He's had money to burn as long as he can remember."

I gave it some thought then snapped:

"Oh, you go! I can't see it matters any more. You have him."

Connie laughed at my pouting mouth. Simm grinned, too.

"Who're you kidding, Giulia. He's not a push-over. He'll make his own mind up whatever we think."

"What exactly do you want him to make his mind up about?" Simm asked in a mild voice. "Or am I missing something here?"

"You're missing something here!" I snapped.

"Is it something Christie could help with?" said Simm, scratching his chin.

Connie's expression lit up. She took his face between her hands and gave him a smacking kiss on the forehead.

"Who's a clever little stepson!" she laughed. "Go home, Giulia. I'll call you when I know something definite."

Simm looked from one to the other of us in confusion, as well might anyone who hadn't lived our history. Christie couldn't even imagine the half of it.

Perhaps that's what Connie had in mind. Perhaps she intended breaking the hold Christie seemed to have over him with a few hard facts.

A tiny little voice at the back of my mind kept repeating over and over 'no chance', but I shook it away on the drive back to Momma's.

Chapter Thirty

A Mother on the Doorstep

Christie

He arrived back at Jiwaku – I'd finally gotten my tongue around it – in a right old state. He flung through the door, donned boots and parka and disappeared towards the mountains via the theater.

I watched him go. He didn't even pause to look down at the men just about completing the construction.

I was a bit non-plussed he didn't even notice the stone mason I had employed to do the finishing work but strode across the nascent blooms in the grass without thought.

There was a time I'd have been worried about his actions, but I knew now, the worst he might do was throw himself off a cliff and there was nothing I could do about that. He'd be back.

I baked some bread and made a good hot casserole for when he returned a few hours later, so he arrived back to warmth and comforting aromas. I didn't often do this - he should appreciate the effort.

"Well?" I said when he returned.

"Well what?" he growled, throwing his parka on the floor and kicking his snow-boots off in a temper. Then he collapsed on his knees, covering his face with his hands.

"I've hurt Giulia beyond bearing. I couldn't stop her crying. I've broken her heart – and her Wedgewood vase." I ask you, who wouldn't smile at that, even inwardly.

Oh, was that all? Women are always singularly unimpressed by the tears of other women. With a man, they are almost always the means to an end.

"Here, get up." I hauled him to his feet by the elbow and urged him towards the kitchen door.

"You'll feel better when you've warmed up a bit and eaten. Then we'll have a proper chat."

I plated up his food and left him to eat while I went to put some laundry away.

When I reappeared, he'd stowed his pots in the dishwasher and looked, if not happy, at least composed. I sat down at the table opposite him and made him look at me.

"Okay – lay it on me."

Harry turned up that evening. He'd moved Barbara, now his wife, and sons up to rented accommodation in town, while the construction was still in progress. He and David were both still touring with their respective bands, but they were getting on now – in their forties like Pa - so they weren't away as often as they used to be. I couldn't see Pa getting away with having the theater to himself. These two were champing at the bit.

The following morning, Pa didn't mention his conversation with Giulia again so I didn't push him.

Instead, he went to inspect the work done while he was away. In such a short time they had managed to achieve so much. Harry had kept them at it until it was too dark to see, laying out the parking lot. For such a delicate-looking man, he sure could crack the whip when he chose.

The workmen were doing their final sweep and packing away their equipment. I stood in the entrance while Pa and Harry chatted to the foreman. Pa was so delighted with the work he shook the man's hand enthusiastically before he left. Then the only sound, thank the Lord, was the gentle tap-tap of the stone mason's hammer as he and his two apprentices worked silently on decorations for the stage surround.

The craftsmen reckoned on a month to finish their work. That would make us nicely on schedule for a July opening. And Pa began to bite his nails.

He telephoned Bobby and asked how the invitation distribution was going.

"Good," said Bobby. "A little over a hundred acceptances so far with a month to go."

Pa released an involuntary sigh of relief.

Harry and David had managed their own distributions so well that no way was Pa going to get away with not giving them their own shows.

A week later Connie turned up looking very apprehensive. I threw my arms around her and dragged her inside, jumping up and down with delight.

"Why didn't you tell me you were coming? I'd have made up a bed and everything. How long will you be staying?"

"Depends on Gil."

Pa was at the theater so didn't see her come. I couldn't imagine how he would react but, what the hell, she was my mother. I had a right to be glad.

I heated up the left-over casserole from the previous day and sat down to chat. Once she'd eaten, she pushed her plate aside and reached over and pulled my long hair out of its plait, stroking it.

"Don't ever cut it," she said. "It seems our troubles began when I cut my hair without telling him. Bit like Samson in reverse."

She sighed and the memories of a lifetime reflected in her eyes.

Chapter Thirty-one

In Which Gil Loses his Temper and Connie Gets a Shock

Christie

My mother stroking my hair made me feel like a child again. She knew how vulnerable and easily hurt I was, which Pa didn't. He'd only seen me when I had a grip on things. But Connie had seen me grieve when Grace died.

She knew losing him would have destroyed me. I think I must have reminded her of Pa in some things. I often acted one way and felt another. Just like Pa had when Jamie absconded and made him responsible for the whole band the year he married Connie.

He'd smiled and cajoled the other guys into keeping going. Then when they left, he went to his room, shut the door and sobbed for an hour.

Connie said he'd never spoken a word of this to anyone. She only knew from Nancy, who had heard him. Then he'd pick himself up until the next disaster, one of which was Connie.

Poor Giulia had been caught in the crossfire. Apart from his music, the one thing Pa couldn't live without was affection. He craved it. She loved him in her own way, but she was a woman-child and would never be strong enough for him. She needed looking after but, unfortunately so did he.

Pa breezed through the door and stopped dead.

"Thanks," said Connie "Nice warm greeting."

I gave her a shove.

"Now, be nice Ma." I said in a failed attempt at levity. "No-one should know better than you he doesn't do surprises."

"OUT!" he yelled.

We both jumped in disbelief, and I made a dive for the door. He grabbed Connie's hand. "Not you."

Naturally I'd made good and sure I'd left the door ajar. No way was I missing this. These were my parents – I was up for giving them a shove in the right direction. I'd think about Giulia later.

"What the fuck are you doing here, Connie. You've never set foot here before. Why now?"

"Answer your own question, genius. I should visit the house my ex-husband shares with his second wife? How does that work?"

Oh, these two should be together. Anger and passion were two sides of the same coin.

There was a pause where I assumed they were both taking deep breaths. Connie began again, making a concerted effort to calm down:

"Giulia came to see me. She couldn't figure out what was going on. I rather assumed she was pretty upset about some vase, though."

'Stupid Connie,' I thought. 'Don't blow it by knocking Giulia. She might be misguided but she's the victim in this.'

It seemed Connie had learned a trick or two from Grace.

"Get out of here, Christie. Mind your own business," she yelled at the near-shut door.

"Never mind her," seethed Pa, dragging Connie past me to the outside door where he threw her coat and boots at her and grabbed his own. "I may be shouting too loud for our daughter's delicate ears in here."

Of course, that was irony. I did 'loud shouting' okay myself as he had good reason to know. But this was pretty thrilling. Who'd have believed they could go at each other like this?

Holding my mother by the arm, he turned to me and glared:

184

"And don't you fucking follow us or I'll…." He never finished the sentence because my mother punched him in the stomach.

They walked to the theater Connie had only heard about from Giulia and Simm. As he dragged her along by the arm, I saw her crane her neck to get a better view of it. He tugged her back. She smacked his hands away and leaned over the parapet above the seats which gave her a splendid view of the whole auditorium.

I was too far away to hear her gasp, but I saw it. She slowly turned and looked Pa square in the eyes without speaking. Before he could stop her, she ran back to the house.

Connie pushed me aside as she entered and made for the phone. She muttered.

"Over my dead body!" or something of the sort.

Pa arrived back a little more slowly, but still out of breath.

'What's she doing NOW!" he asked aghast. I got the feeling he'd spent most of his life being aghast at Connie.

"Making all your dreams come true, I suspect,"

I felt so smug but I thought he was going to expire at her next sentence.

'Giulia. Get on the first plane and get here now. To hell with your mother's charity fund raisers. Tell her you've a fault in the electricity… hell, tell her the whole freakin' place has burned to the ground – but get here yesterday!"

My mother the Valkyrie.

Once they'd bawled each other out it all went a bit flat. Pa and drank coffee and Connie had a very large tumbler of Pa's bourbon ration. Then someone, not sure who, said:

"Let's go check out the theater." So we did.

Early flowering crocuses dotted the banking on both sides of the entrance. I thought the parking lot could do with some attention but it was overhung in places with the remains of pink honeysuckle vines which had wrapped round trees on the edge of the lot. These could look great. I'd gotten so into plans for the theatre, I couldn't shut off.

The entrance had been fitted with a wrought-iron security gate. Pa had to nip back to the house for the key, which gave Connie and I chance for a private chat.

"Have you always got on this well?" I asked

"Don't be impertinent. No – we can do much better than this. Give us time."

"When he comes back, look at him. Take a really good look and tell yourself what you see. Not me – you. I already know."

"You have absolutely no idea of our history, Christie. You don't know why we are as we are – all three of us, Gil, Giulia and me. This tangle goes back nearly twenty-five years."

"Oh, shit Connie! I don't need to know about your past. That's gone. It's your present and future I'm concerned with. What does it matter that you hit each other over the head with iron bars when you were twenty?"

Connie actually looked relieved when Pa reappeared brandishing a large rather ornate key and fitted it in the lock. The door creaked as it swung open. That needed to go on the 'to do' list.

From the center of the auditorium the view was spectacular, as if it had been carved by Titans.

I saw Connie looking at him covertly from time to time. I hope she saw what I saw.

Here was a man bursting with the spirit of love, a man with his dreams coming true before his eyes. Now that he'd learned to forget himself, he'd found his true desires all around him. All thoughts of the past had been swept away by a yearning for the future so strong it filled his eyes with tears. Who wouldn't want to be part of that?

We wandered up and down the steps between the banks of seating. Close up, a thread of quartzite made the stone shimmer. I turned and saw Pa spinning round and round on the stage with his arms extended, looking up at the sky. Then he launched into a verse of the song he loved so much.

"They asked me how I knew,

My true love was true.

I of course replied...."

His barrel chest heaved, and his voice resonated round the auditorium, bouncing off the stone and reverberating through the air. There certainly would be limited need of speakers.

He suddenly stopped and turned to look at Connie. I may as well not have been there.

She was crying and his face was filled with such awful pain. She turned and ran back to the house.

I put my arms round his waist and said:

"Oh Pa, I'm sorry. This is one addiction I can do nothing about."

He kissed my hair and when I looked up he had recovered enough to smile.

"I know, darling. It's been going on so long it would feel odd without it."

187

He annoyed me so much with this passive acceptance. I'd had to combat it at the start of our time together. I pushed away.

"Oh, stop being such a fucking hippie and do something about it. This is not the time for 'peace and love'. Do something."

I marched off across the auditorium in a fury, convinced I came from a line of idiots.

Giulia turned up the following morning, lip out, and flounced through the cathedral room where Pa was standing by the window with Connie. She shouldered between them and said to Connie:

"Well, what the hell is so important you've dragged me here? I guess he..." she motioned over her shoulder with her thumb, "...gave his version of our last meeting. Could it be you want mine?"

Suddenly Pa had ceased to exist for both of them.

"You know that's crap, Giulia! I'm more likely to get your version than his – from him. He'll have bent over backwards to understand."

"Well, this is one situation when he couldn't have found it much of a stretch."

'Nope', I thought from my perch near the fire, 'probably true'.

My mother huffed and, grabbing Giulia's hand, dragged her back outside.

"You come too," she shouted over her shoulder to Pa and began the walk to the theater door, now standing wide, never once releasing Giulia's hand.

"Right..." she said, dragging Giulia halfway up a bank of seating, "sit down."

I stayed by the door - I wasn't getting involved.

"You..." she ordered Gil. "Do what you did yesterday. Nothing else. Just that."

Pa's look implored her not to do this. Both women ignored him.

"Do it," Connie said through clenched teeth.

As he began, the notes sparkling in the morning air, he forgot his situation and lost himself in his oneness with nature. It was spellbinding.

I noticed with complete shock that the two women were holding tightly onto each other's hands. Then Giulia turned, kissed Connie on the cheek and shook her head. Smiling tearfully, she quietly left. Pa carried on singing, oblivious.

For the very first time I understood the love which had existed between all three of these wonderful people for decades. I understood the crippling pain and prayed to God to let me be a part of the healing.

Once Pa came back to earth, and realized the world had turned in his absence, I walked over and gave him a hug.

"See ya lata aligata," I whispered in his ear. I winked broadly at Connie on the way out.

I didn't see them for two days, then they wandered into the cathedral room like two moon-struck teens, clasping hands and gazing into each other's eyes. Well, maybe that was a bit of an exaggeration, but Pa didn't even notice when he tripped over a rug and Connie had to hold him upright.

It should have been absolutely nauseating but it wasn't. Frankly, it was such a freakin' relief it was blissful.

There was only one course of action for me. I packed a bag and went to stay at my new possession in San Clemente. No doubt they'd call when they resurfaced.

Chapter Thirty-two
Harry and David Astonished (In a Good Way)

Christie

A large part of day one I spent with Maurice discussing security issues for Jiwaku. It was his field of expertise, so I ended up listening to him rather than giving him instructions. I told him what we'd agreed about using the workmen. We settled on a price, and I left it in his capable hands.

His daughter Betty had done wonders with 'her bit of soil'. The gardener had allowed her to keep expanding it until it filled the whole of the front of their cottage with brilliant color.

When Pa hadn't called after three days, I began to get a bit bored. If we didn't get on with things, the opening would have to be put back.

I rang Harry and David. Harry was away but David drove over from L.A. the following day, toting a towel and swim shorts.

'C'mon! All work and no play… Let's go get wet."

You couldn't help liking him. He didn't smile much, but when he did the sun came out.

So I donned my bikini, wound my hair round my head and we made for the beach.

He refused to go the surf side of the pier, so we ended up amongst the buckets and spades at the other side.

The water was just heavenly, warm and smooth as silk on my skin. I dipped my head beneath the surface, watching my breath bubble upwards. I closed my eyes. Paradise.

"Thank you, Davy. I needed that – it's been a really fraught week. A REALLY fraught week."

I rolled my eyes.

"I know," he said with a straight face. "The right rear hub cap fell off my car. Calamity, right?"

"Let's go grab a beer," he grinned. "We need to chat about what comes next at that place with the unpronounceable name – can't you do something about that?"

Instead, we went back to Ginsling, got a beer each from the cooler and spread the plans out on the table.

"I at least have to look as if I've been doing something until Harry gets back."

He'd been immersed in the whole project from the beginning.

"I've left the details of security in the hands of Maurice. He does the same job here. He's reliable and has good contacts. The ball is in your court after that. The music needs sorting between you Harry and Pa, if I can get him out of bed with Connie."

This came as something of a shock. He straightened his spine and looked at me with his mouth wide.

"You're shittin' me! After decades? And him married to Giulia! What the hell happened?"

"The theater. Giulia and Pa were tugging in opposite directions and Giulia lost. More than the house."

"Goddamn, what a relief! You have no idea how that man' suffered. When he and Connie divorced, Harry and I didn' think he'd survive. Thank God.

"Then neither Connie nor Giulia would let him get to you which broke him up even more."

192

He was a lovely man, so he was quick to add, somewhat unnecessarily,

"A bitch for Giulia though."

"I think, in the end, it came as a relief. She'd been holding them together – against all odds – for almost the whole time. It must have been exhausting as well as heartbreaking, She and Connie more or less shook on it. At least, she walked away with her head held high. The arrogant bastard'll dine out on that for years."

I could say that with impunity because it was so far from the truth as to be ridiculous.

"Don't go anywhere," he said and dashed into the house for the nearest phone.

"Hi, Barb. Harry there? Oh shit, I forgot he was away. Tell him to call..." he paused to look at the dial "…361-2113. Its urgent. Very urgent."

He slammed the phone down, ran back onto the terrace and sank half his bottle of beer in one swallow.

"We need to get down to work. Call your Pa until he answers - all day if necessary. We've to move now or we won't be ready. There's new material to rehearse – well, for me anyway."

"Pa has a stack to the ceiling. He's been writing every spare moment since the theater was started. Until three days ago, that is."

The phone rang.

"Shit, that's quick, even for Harry!"

It was Pa. He sounded deliriously happy which was obvious even over the phone. I think at that moment, if I'd asked for the Cullinan Diamond, he'd have found a way to get it to me.

"David's here. He thinks you should get started on the music.

Harry's away at the moment, but David shouted so loud down the phone at Barbara I think she got the message it was urgent."

Pa started to reply then broke off. Why, was obvious – and becoming embarrassing.

"Oh, for fuck's sake, go take a shower. You can't be doing that when there are people around."

"She's right," said a breathless Connie in the background.

"We'll be back as soon as Harry gets here. Get the cottage together." I put the phone down.

"Did you know you'd gone red?" laughed David.

The phone rang again and this time it was Harry. David explained the situation but left out the bit about Connie and Gil until just before he put down the receiver. I poked Davy in the ribs and made him call back.

Harry, nearly choking with shock, said they were in New York but he expected to be back in Riverside in two days, he'd have a couple of days at home then be over. Thoughtful man. But, in view of David's news I did wonder if he wouldn't be there earlier.

"Best part of a week," worried David, biting his lip. "I'll go back to L.A. and hand out more tickets - sorry invitations."

Half an hour later he was gone.

I decided to stay at Ginsling - just loved that, it was so Grace - for a couple more days rather than be a third wheel at Jiwaku. Hopefully, by then they might be able to prize away from each other for short periods.

So there would be three extra cars parked in the parking lot in the mountains five days later. I banged on the door rather than use my key, just to be on the safe side. Connie opened it looking

194

all rosy.

I cornered Pa coming out of the kitchen, dragged him back inside and threatened him.

"I expect you to behave in a considerate manner to everybody here. Put your girlfriend down for a few hours and concentrate on what we're all here for."

He still looked as if he'd been hit over the head with a hammer but at least when he answered he was reasonably coherent.

"Promise." He threw his arms around me and danced me round in a circle.

"Oh shit. Stop it or I'll put a crate of beer and a dozen bottles of Jack in here to give us some peace."

There was a time he wouldn't have found that in the least funny.

I straightened my t-shirt and looked grumpy although all I wanted to do was feel glad for them both. He knew it and grinned.

"Come on. Let's go see if I can behave."

He and Connie shared a moment of hilarity at my expense, before they were both engulfed in a bear hug from a delighted Harry who could only manage:

"Oh man…. oh, jeez… oh that's just the greatest!" Hardly Shakespeare.

Then Pa said, "Come on, guys. Put your gear in the SUV and we'll go down to the cottage."

That left me alone with my mother. I must have looked defensive because she laughed and took my arm.

"Come on let's take a walk. You look as if you could do with some fresh air."

195

"You're right. I just found out why babies aren't born with the faculty of understanding."

We took the path up the slope past the theater and spread below us was a meadow bejeweled with summer flowers. The mountain air was invigorating and the sun warm on our faces.

She was past forty years old but she ran down the hill like a child, the flowers to her waist.

"Come on," she said and continued running to a small brook at the bottom of the slope, shook off her sandals and splashed around in the icy water. When her feet were too cold, we sat in a hollow, hidden by drifts of flowers while she made daisy-chains. Her joy was infectious and filled my heart to bursting.

And suddenly, the mother I'd known as Auntie Connie for most of my life was my friend. I grabbed handfuls of flowers and wove them in a coronet which I set on her hair. She could never have looked lovelier. Her skin was like a girl's. Her hair, still black as ebony, bound with bright blue columbine and blowing in the breeze. She looked like a bride.

The guys were walking back up the drive for a lunch break when we burst round the corner and almost knocked them down.

Gill was awe-struck. Their second marriage, for such it was, was reason enough for leaving them alone for a while.

"An hour," I yelled after them as they entered the house.

The rest of us ate pizza.

Chapter Thirty-three
God-Given Creativity

Gil

I had fallen in love with my darling all over again. Only this was not a boy's love rooted in desire. This was the love of a man whose very cells craved her body, spirit and soul.

Each time I lost myself in her velvet eyes, I saw my devotion reflected back.

What the hell had we done? I'd left her alone when all she wanted was her husband. And it took our wonderful, our unique daughter to show it to us.

She'd pushed and worried at us until we'd abandoned our terror of rejection and taken a step in the dark. But our private time really had to come to an end. The world had to be faced again and what a joy that could – would – be.

Harry, David and I had decided to have a show each sharing the instrumentals and backing vocals for the lead. The songs would all be new, and in no way based on our bands. This was liberation.

All the arrangements had necessarily to be simple and based on live performance. I'd even get to play some raw rock and roll. That had always been Jamie's thing. My voice was too smooth, but I'd find a way.

Christie didn't know yet that - a. she was writing lyrics for one, me, and collaborating with two others and - b. she was playing piano for all three of us. I looked forward to telling her. She was fine with her university gigs but backing Harry Forster, Davy Ellis and Gil Robson would petrify her.

Also, Bobby would be up in a couple of days. I was looking

forward to that too. It would be good for Connie to spend time with her him.

Oh, life was just so good!

We three guys had to work out some discipline in the little cottage. I was used to working alone with my papers spread out all over the floor. Obviously, that had to stop.

I brought down a two-piece nest of tables someone had pushed away in a garden shed, dusted them down and the other guys used them. There was a bigger dining table for stacking finished or pending compositions. I squatted on the floor as usual.

I liked to work out basic shapes on a keyboard – easier than guitar. I had a few of these noted down already – just enough to remind me.

Once past the keyboard stage, we'd work with the guitars in our own rooms at the house, slipping out now and then to check something on the cathedral room piano.

We got off to a dishearteningly slow start while we figured out ways of initially working together in the same room. But within the week we had it nailed.

Bobby had arrived. After a bit of family discussion, including news of their Mom's family in Kailua, they settled into an easy affection it was a pleasure to see.

The days were passing fast, and I was beginning to worry we wouldn't make it on time.

We'd planned on the first week in July, but it now looked as if it would be nearer the fourteenth or fifteenth.

Then, all of a sudden, the whole place was buzzing.

Maurice had arranged for the installation of three portable cabins. One, placed to the rear of the entrance, was for the use of his security staff; one to the side of the stage as a dressing room for us. The last and largest one, for instruments and equipment placed next to the dressing room. Maurice arranged a twenty-four-hour guard.

Then our friends started to get involved. We found we had more help than we could possibly use. Our work-guy had it right. There were electricians, construction workers, woodworkers, musicians, a man who tuned pianos for a living and just so many other useful people. All our friends, all on our side, all wanting us to do good.

I made sure I wrote a special love song to sing to Connie. It took hours to write because I had to get it just right. I had to haul Christie in to help with the words, because my version was beginning to be very 'moon in June', which was not what I wanted at all.

"You don't have to start from scratch. Why don't you take some already written lyrics and twist them to what you want? For example, "My love Has Come Along" – my favorite Etta James song.

"'At last, my love has come along' could become 'Our souls are one again, at last' or something of the sort."

That became:

I heard you laughing in the mountain air

Smelled your perfume on the breeze

The softness of a whispered plea

Never, never leave.

Nothing the same but that was the idea. Not exactly brilliant but unless you were Paul Simon, they rarely were. Connie would understand. Her face was before me with every word written.

I sang it to Harry and David and they were silent for a few moments then Davy clapped. Such an accolade from that accomplished musician. I would work on it some more, but it was pretty much finished. Harry asked if he could sing backing, he had ideas for harmonies.

We wove songs together and worked individually, and by the end of the first week in July, we had a good play-list to check out in the theater. The stone gave it the most spectacular acoustics, or perhaps the spirit of our music made it so.

Most of my songs had electric guitar accompaniments, which I did. David would help with vocals and some more dynamic keyboards, and Harry with some acoustic guitar, but mostly vocals. Christie was on piano. I'd yet to break it to her she was about to become a professional, if unpaid, rock pianist.

Bobby would fill in on anything else – he had become a complete all-rounder through filling in gaps in 'California Crystal' as needed. He was especially great when Jamie died and, although he didn't have Jamie's showmanship, he made a pretty good job of laying down a beat on his drums. He was good on electric keyboards as well.

"Christie, my sweet…," I began.

"What do you want?" she asked wryly. We'd a good father/daughter relationship.

"Harry and Davy have something they want to ask you."

My two friends stood in the doorway looking nervous.

"If you have something to ask Pa, you ask it and don't lay it on them."

I took a deep breath. "We'd like you to play for us at our concerts."

200

"Glad to."

Oh shit! I could never tell, even now, which way she would jump.

The day before the planned date I began to really panic. Hordes of people started arriving. Some I recognized, some I didn't - some Harry and Davy didn't know either. The cat was out of the bag - anything could happen. It looked as if all our hard work had been for nothing.

I sent Christie to speak to Maurice. Apparently, he'd sent a large contingent of his security guys to mingle with the crowd, checking invitations and evicting those who had no right to be there. He also had men stationed in the woods.

That evening our people set up camp on the edge of the parking lot. It was a mini-Woodstock, set amongst honeysuckle garlands and overhanging cottonwood. Giulia would have been horrified, but I found Connie sitting amongst half a dozen people of her own age eating – of all things – a huge slice of pumpkin pie and laughing.

I stood back and watched her until she caught sight of me leaning against a pine. She smiled and the whole world receded. There were just the two of us, standing by the steps of the Giordano house in Los Angeles, when she was sixteen, and as shy as a fawn.

"Oh fuck, Pa. Wake up! They want you in the instruments cabin. Davy has a problem with…something or other."

She dashed off on another errand.

Before I left, I kissed my girl lightly on the lips and introduced to her new friends. I went to find out what David wanted.

Then it was all done. All the planning and rehearsing. All the doubt and uncertainty. All gone, and before us a theater filled with faces, many I recognized. Harry and David were walking between the seats kissing cheeks and shaking hands, sharing a joke here, a serious conversation there.

I began to recognize my own beloved people. A lady with bright blue eyes who had sat in the front seat of many of our shows since I was a boy. I learned her name was Susan Williams from Baltimore. She'd brought her grown-up son and daughter.

There was a man with a guitar pick with my name on it tucked in the band of his hat. He shook my hand fervently and told me my music had been the backdrop to his entire life. I was truly humbled. This was something I had never heard locked away in my Ivory Tower. I gave him another couple of picks from my pocket and clapped him on the back.

A man in his forties with a twenty-year-old wife, blonde, chirpy and obviously overawed. I went and shook hands. Her eyes nearly popped out of her head. The guy was Greg. I'd seen him often over the footlights, part of a seething mass of humanity. He was English.

I also saw past band members. They smiled and waved, happy I remembered them. How could I forget?

Every so often, someone offered me an album or a book to sign, but no-one pushed or jostled. These were my friends.

The three of us, Harry, Davy and I, ended up standing at the entrance, greeting our guests as they handed in their invitations.

Strangers laughed and joked together, sharing stories and singing snatches of our old songs.

Then everyone was seated. I saw Connie with Barbara Forster in the front row. I was so strung out by being on stage without the band I momentarily froze, which I covered by adjusting my mic. Connie smiled sweetly and winked. Then she looked at the others on stage to show I wasn't alone.

202

We started with a rocker to get things going. I was mortified that the audience clapped politely but weren't exactly ecstatic. All the songs were new – I just hoped they weren't expecting the same old stuff. Christie hopped over from the piano, covered the mic and whispered in my ear:

"Too 'Crystal'. Do one of the soft ones. They want to hear your voice."

As she scooted back to the piano she mouthed 'four' to the others and held up four fingers, meaning the altered set number for the next song. She started into the intro, Bobby picked up a soft rhythm and I played the sweet melody on my guitar.

Once I began to sing, everything dropped into place. When I opened my eyes again, I found my head was tilted upwards and I was gazing at a heaven full of brilliant stars. There was deathly silence – you could have heard a pin drop.

Then it began. The whole stadium was on its feet, cheering and whistling. They were so close to me I could see tears glistening on cheeks and expressions so loving they made me gasp. I'd been doing this for thirty years and had never, never seen this before.

Even more amazing, everyone on stage had put down their instruments and were applauding too. I looked round, so overcome with emotion, it took me some time to whisper into the microphone:

"Thank you, thank you, my friends."

We closed the set with my song to Connie. I looked into her eyes and sang every word directly to her. At the end, I looked at an audience filled with quiet emotion. It seemed only natural to put down my guitar, run across the stage and pull her up beside me. She was horrified and hid her head in my shoulder.

My dearest friends. I want you to know Connie, the love of my life. We lost each other for a while so I wrote this song from my

203

heart just for her."

Connie was crying and absolutely rigid in my arms.

Two fingers poked each of us hard in the back and a voice hissed:

"Connie stop being so fucking pathetic and Pa, there are other people in the room, pull yourself together."

Oh, thank God…thank God for Christie. Connie and I both shouted out loud with laughter.

"And this is our darling daughter, Christie – builder of dreams."

I'd never seen her speechless before. I licked my finger and drew a number one in the air. She threw back her head and laughed out loud.

The audience cheered and cheered.

We didn't stick around for an encore. There wasn't time. We only had fifteen minutes to wash change and retune instruments. This last came as something of a surprise, since we'd all been decades having technicians to do it for us. It took me back to childhood.

During the second half, Davy and Harry tried out a couple of numbers they were unsure of. I saw Harry nod to himself as a chord he'd been struggling with suddenly fell into place.

In all truth, there was nothing, absolutely nothing I could have wanted more, or so I thought.

My new style was loved by my friends – I had worried myself sleepless over that – Connie was by my side and my daughter my soulmate. What could have been better? But there was one thing. And I got that too.

The last song I sang was the only one which wasn't a new-write

It was the song which for so many, many years I had sung at every single concert solely for my friends. Sometimes I had had to fight tooth and nail with the other guys in the band, who thought it had become a drag, and everyone was sick and tired of it. But about this one thing I was adamant.

And tonight was no exception, I was surrounded by people who were my life's companions.

As soon as the intro struck up, they all stood and cheered loudly. This was the one song I never lost myself in. This was theirs's. As always, I sang directly to them, letting my eyes rove over the shining faces and feeling my own wreathed in smiles. We communicated on a level too high for words.

Then the impossible happened.

As I was gazing out into the crowd, catching this eye and that, my attention was drawn to one particular pair of hazel eyes, crinkled at the corners and shining with love. I stopped singing mid-song and just stared and stared.

So many times I'd heard him, but Christie was the only one he'd ever shown himself to.

She was behind me in seconds.

"Keep going. I see him too. He didn't come to see you freeze mid-song like an amateur."

The audience was beginning to get restive, so I apologized and picked up where I'd left off, never taking my eyes off a face I never thought I'd see again this side of heaven. Jamie, my beloved brother Jamie. He gave the A-okay sign and began to clap along in time, mouthing the words, his eyes sparkling with delight, shaking his long sun-streaked hair in time to the music like he used to.

He was sitting halfway up an empty stairway so I could see him quite clearly, but I knew no-one else could…. except Christie.

Even Connie didn't know he was there.

As the song ended. he turned and did an arm-pump and blew me a kiss. Then he skipped down the stairs where he put his arm round a petite fair-haired woman with a kindly face and squeezed her with enthusiasm.

My Mom looked up at him smiling that smile which always gave me comfort. Then they were gone, disappearing into the shadows near the entrance.

I looked about me and felt one with the universe. I was surrounded by the people who cared for me most in the whole world. Connie, Christie and Bobby, Harry and David, my beloved audience. All surrounded by the majesty of the mountains and the overwhelming arc of the star-spangled night sky. And music enfolded me in its wings.

The audience was standing in silence, so I walked up and down the steps, shaking hands, kissing the cheeks of strangers. And the air crackled about us.

When I returned to the stage, I invited Harry and Davy to share my mic. I even invited Christie but she didn't, thank God.

"Please sing the last song along with me. It's ours but I've never heard you sing it - I would be so honored if …."

Christie cut me off with the first notes of the intro before I got too maudlin. Harry and David's voices covered my initial broken notes.

Christie stopped playing and only voices rose in the air, pure and so loud the mountains rang.

Chapter Thirty-four
Two Ghosts and a House Naming

Connie

The audience left in small groups, laughing and talking, excited by the magic of the evening. I heard cars slowly begin to roll down the drive to the pitch-dark road. Only then did they start their engines and disappear into the night.

There was one thing I saw I don't think anyone else did, certainly not Gil and Christie. For some reason Gil had stopped playing mid-song and was staring fixedly at the stairs to his right. Christie was beside him in seconds, whispering in his ear with that well-known determined expression on her face. He apologized to the audience and picked up where he'd left off.

While they were distracted, out of the corner of my eye I saw two figures standing to the side of the wall near the entrance. I couldn't say why, but I was impelled to check them out closely. There was a sudden flash of tiny sparkles as she moved and gestured to her companion. I was astonished to realize it was Giulia, with a young man who had his arm around her slender shoulders. She smiled at me and put her finger to her lips.

When Gil began to sing again, I turned away, and by the end of the song when I looked back, they were gone.

Christie and I went back to the house and left the guys returning the instruments to the cabin. We'd finish clearing up in the morning. Tonight, we were so exhausted we just wanted to fall into bed.

As I went up the steps, wearily dragging my feet, I saw the name plaque next to the door and ran my fingers over the incised letters.

"Who put this here?" I asked Christie. She shrugged.

"Giulia and Pa called it Mon Repose. Pa got flak from all directions so he renamed it. Why?"

A soft voice behind us said:

"Beat it, Christie."

He held my eyes for a few seconds then said:

"I named it just for you." Then he walked away.

I was weeping so hard when I returned to the house that Christie wondered what was going on.

"He has an uncanny knack for opening his mouth and putting both feet in it," she said.

"You know I'm half Hawaiian?" Christie nodded. "The name of the house is 'Jiwaku'. It means 'My Soul'. He said he named it for me."

Christie looked unimpressed. I was so overawed but thought perhaps, on reflection, we might have to sit down and figure something a bit more poetic than 'Jiwaku'. Enchanted though I was by the gesture, it did sound like a board game.

We headed to our own rooms.

A while after, I felt a warm body slide beneath the covers and hold me in his arms. That was how we slept that first night and for countless after, my head against his heart. Sound and dreamless, exhausted and happy beyond measure.

Epilogue – Part One

Christie

I am older now, but I suspect little wiser.

My own granddaughter lies sleeping in her crib beside my chair. She is a tiny delicate thing with her grandfather's perfect nose and her mother's golden hair, a halo round her head.

Dad had been right. I showed more affection for Pa and Connie than I ever had for him and Mom, which was a tragedy for all three of us.

Kind as he was, I think Pa secretly found comfort from that for the eighteen years we were apart. Nevertheless, he insisted Mom and Dad visit often and was quick to admonish me when I forgot them, which I'm afraid I did quite often. Mom tried desperately not to show her sadness to Connie, which was difficult since Connie was unable to hide her own 'joie de vivre'. She had everything she'd ever dreamed of.

Connie still lives, still beautiful in her seventies, desperate for the love she lost when Pa joined his beloved brother five years ago.

She and Pa lived the rest of their lives together in an idyll of caring which gradually obliterated the sadness of their separation and guilt over their treatment of Giulia.

Giulia may have been delicate to look at but she was one tough cookie when it came to business – her father had been right. She sold the apartment block in Denver at an obscene profit and moved back to live with her mother in Beverly Hills. Within a year she had resumed her Giordano name and family ties.

I think she was happy enough. There were big spreads in the society press when she remarried a couple of years later. Not to Tom, but to someone with a private jet and a family name. Needless to say no invitation landed on the Robson mat.

We get a Christmas card from her every year with a scribbled note inside. She and her husband moved to Hawaii where she gave birth to twins. How the hell someone that size carried two babies to term is a mystery.

It still makes me emotional when I see the gold chain, with a pendant in the shape of the blue mountain columbines fashioned from pale sapphires and yellow diamonds – a precious flower like the ones I placed on her hair when their love was first rekindled.

He gave the necklace to her on their tenth anniversary after he'd tried everything he knew with zero success, to coerce her into remarrying him. She'd refused point blank saying she couldn't remarry someone she'd never unmarried.

My own medallion is still in place around my throat. I swore I'd never take it off unless either Gil or Connie asked me to. I see Connie check it out every now and then and her face lights with love but not for me.

In the fullness of time, I married Rob Anderson - a wonderful man, the son of one of Pa's special friends. Perhaps I should tell our story sometime – it would fill a book on its own.

Pa and Connie dressed me in finest China silk lace, and a trailing veil held in place with a band of tiny diamond florets. I have it still, wrapped in tissue in a box in my closet.

My bouquet was all Connie's own work. A cascade of old-fashioned cream and blush roses tied in ivory silk ribbon. It was so profuse it reached the hem of my dress. When Pa saw it, his face lit up and he kissed Connie like a boy with his first love. I suppose there must have been a reason hidden long ago in their past because Connie gazed at him and blushed like the roses.

When I came to put on my lip-gloss, and check my appearance for the final time, placed neatly on my dressing table amongst the plethora of makeup items, was a small abalone and white gold box. When I carefully raised the lid, it contained the bracelet of dew-drop diamonds in a spider's web setting Giulia so often wore. The first time I saw it I was thirteen years old. Attached was a note:

A small token of my love, dearest Christie

on this your special day.

Your friend forever - Giulia

She'd left without being seen, like the wood nymph I once took her for.

If I hadn't been wearing mascara, I'd have wept. As it was I sat down, thanking God I hadn't put my veil on yet.

I asked Connie if she would mind me wearing the bracelet on my wedding day. She said, as she had all the happiness in the world, she could spare a little for someone else. She clasped it round my wrist herself.

"Don't worry about Pa. I'll let him know so he doesn't have the vapors on the church steps. Be prepared. Your nerves are nothing to his. You'd think it was his wedding."

"Bad as that?"

"Oh worse.... much worse." She looked heavenward, and we both burst out laughing.

Connie brushed my long hair until it shone then twisted it into a chignon on my nape. She waited until we arrived at church before putting on my veil, flouncing it out so it floated in the air.

Pa chose that very instant to walk out of the church doors and stopped in his tracks. He didn't move a muscle for a full minute but ran his eyes over me from head to foot, so many times I began to think my dress was caught in my panties.

He lifted my veil and kissed me gently on the lips.

"God knew what he was doing when he blessed me with you, Christie. I'll thank him all my days."

He replaced my veil and passed my hand to Dad to walk me down the aisle.

Rob and I were blessed with a son and daughter, Jamie and Katrina, who from birth was called Trina.

Mothers always think their children are the most beautiful beings on the planet but mine really were.

Jamie had his name-sake's hazel eyes and thick, unruly hair. Also, his ready wit and irreverent humor.

His grandpa taught him to play a pretty mean guitar. He also taught him what he could of singing, as he had tried once with me, but he'd inherited my genes in the vocal department which was perhaps as well. Everyone would fall short of Gil Robson's heavenly voice.

Trina was little and quick like a sprite and just as naughty. She had her grandpa's nose and cloud-blue eyes and had him wrapped round her little finger from the first day he saw her.

He spoiled her shamelessly.

Until the day, when she was five years old, an angel came for our angel. Trina died of leukemia.

I found Pa in the theater breaking guitar after guitar against the stone steps, sobbing out loud and cursing God at the top of his voice. We held each other shaking, until the pain became bearable, then went back indoors. I think he lost a little of his soul that day, and his spirit took time to grow back again no matter how many candles he lit.

Harry passed away last Spring. Of all the stupid things, he was electrocuted plugging a new guitar into an amp.

Harry had looked after me for Pa and been his dear trusted friend since they were kids together, playing high school hops. He never gave up touring and called to see Pa when he could.

Davy got bored with his band once he saw what Pa had accomplished. We never got rid of him – still haven't - because he fills the theater with the fans who had become true friends, most of whom he is on first name terms with, at every given opportunity. He bullied Pa and Harry into appearing too, so Pa was never allowed to retire. His love of music and his audiences never diminished.

Until Pa died, the three of them would often ride over the mountains to the magical crystal land that was Crestone. I don't think the other two got much out of it, but they enjoyed the ride and the exercise. Pa came back like a recharged battery.

They got to know Anukula's wife and family as friends. The children now have families of their own, but only one ever left Crestone.

A grown-up Jacob and Mylo came often to stay at Jiwaku, now renamed 'Ginsling' in memory of Grace. Jacob never married, but eventually Mylo brought his wife and daughters for visits.

Mylo once asked me if I thought it was their fault Pa and Connie divorced. We had been watching Pa having fun throwing his little daughter into the air and catching her until the baby was so bounced around she deposited her dinner on Pa's beard. I don't believe I ever did answer his question – we were both hysterical with laughter at the look on Pa's face. But I felt the sadness in Mylo at what he'd missed.

The words 'dither' and 'rock star' you wouldn't have thought had much connection, but my rock star Pa turned up one afternoon having tramped through a couple of inches of powdery snow and stood on our doorstep looking anywhere but at me. I pulled him inside.

He didn't speak - just handed me a cream parchment envelope. The card inside read

Mr. Richard and Mrs. Caroline Webster

Request the pleasure of the company of

Mr. Gil Robson and Mrs. Connie Robson

At the wedding of their daughter Rosalind to Mr. Simeon Maxwell

He looked as if he was waiting for the apocalypse as I read it through.

"Well?" I asked, turning the card over just to make sure I hadn't missed anything on the back.

"But he didn't invite you. We thought you'd be devastated."

Growing up I had often questioned the sanity of the adults in my family. It seemed they hadn't improved with age.

"You mean you thought I'd be upset that Simm hadn't invited his ex-fiancé to his wedding? I'm sure the bride would have loved that!"

The wedding was held at the Webster's family home somewhere in Connecticut and I later learned from Pa, Simm and his new wife had moved to Germany and he was working as an export agent for Porsche. There was something in the name that horrified Connie and made Pa glower.

I prayed to the Spirit of all good things that Simeon's life would be as happy as mine had been, and that Richard Webster would be the father he never had.

Deborah didn't outlive her teens. In the end, her character made her life insupportable, even for herself.

So Oliver was left alone and is still so far as I know. We never saw him again in LA or San Clemente and Connie would have known had he turned up at Windham.

Rob and I stayed in Colorado so I could be near Connie and Pa. I told him they were both feckless and couldn't do without me, which was partially true I suppose. The second one anyway.

As the years passed Connie developed arthritis in her right knee. It wasn't bad but it put paid to the frequent walks she took in the mountains with Pa. It made me sad to see how much they both missed strolling together hand in hand in the clear air.

He did try his best, but we all saw him glance out of the cathedral room window when he thought no-one was looking, and one morning Connie found him watching the sun burst over the horizon at dawn. She tiptoed away – he never knew she'd seen.

It made her adamant he wouldn't lose his delight in the mountains, so she gave me one or two tactless shoves and coerced me into going instead.

Epilogue - Part Two

Christie

One day, as we had climbed quite high and Pa had become tired, we sat on rocks overlooking a steep gully. It had been grey and dismal when we'd set out, but he was unusually insistent I go with him. I was glad I did, because the leaden skies turned from misty grey to silver to bright blue in a couple of hours.

It was a walk we took often, so neither of us felt much need for conversation, and sat and observed the vista lost in our own thoughts. Then he said:

"Christie, I don't want you to contradict or argue with me, but I want you to do precisely what I ask. Think you can do that?"

At one time I'd have tweaked his beard and told him not to be such a condescending old person or something less polite. But, somehow, it didn't seem appropriate that day. He looked as he always did but there was an expression in his eyes I couldn't quite fathom, so I nodded and waited for him to continue.

"I have good reason to pay a visit to Crestone. Davy has agreed to come with me, but I don't want either you or your mother there."

"Too bad!" I said as a reflex action, then I remembered what I'd promised, and held my tongue muttering 'sorry'.

"It isn't anything you've done. I need to see Anukula's family about something. I'm asking you to be patient and not ask questions of Davy either. This is between him and me."

I was absolutely mystified and followed him down the hillside not a little alarmed. After a few yards, he pulled my hand through his arm and began, oddly, to sing a jaunty song about birds on branches.

If I hadn't been looking directly at him, I'd have missed a fleeting glance. It was a mixture of fear, anxiety and overwhelming sadness but was gone almost as quickly as it had appeared. If it was anyone but my Pa, I'd have thought I'd imagined it. But we had always had a sixth sense about each other's feelings, so I knew I'd been right.

I started to speak but he put a gloved finger over my lips and continued our walk. After a few moments of silence, he said:

"Precisely three days after I leave, I want you to bring Connie to Crestone. It must be exactly three days. Do you understand?"

He could see I was on the point of a complete meltdown, so he put his arm round me.

"You are the second most important thing to happen in my entire life. In some ways you are *the* most important thing of all because you and I share things Connie could never understand. I want you to know I love you and nothing – nothing – will ever come between us. There will be times you might doubt my word on that. Don't. Things will become clear in the fullness of time."

I was devastated.

"Pa…. why won't you tell me? We've always shared everything. You're frightening me. Tell me, please."

"It's not my secret to tell, darling….." Oh hell, not that old turkey again.

A couple of days later, David came and they drove to the stables together. I watched the car disappear round the corner at the bottom of the drive.

My fear had subsided over the past couple of days and I was starting to get mad.

"Where the fuck is he going?" I asked Connie in the vain hope she might know something I didn't. But she was as mystified as me. I then became angry on her behalf as well. I stormed out of the house with no idea where I was going.

I ended up in the theater. It hadn't been used for a while and old leaves had drifted into corners. It seemed strange, empty and silent almost spooky. I sat on one of the front seats and looked about me. It was *completely* empty. Not even an echo of laughter or love, music or cheering friends. Just a grey empty shell, which belonged to the mountains and had only been lent to us for a speck of time. I shivered and wrapped my arms about me.

I turned to go and glanced a silent figure sitting not six rows back. Jamie. Of course.

He was smiling ear to ear. Shit, he was annoying! Here we were sitting on this terminally depressing hunk of rock and he still found something to be cheerful about!

"What are you doing here, dumbass? Go haunt someone else."

Which only sent him off into peels of silent laughter.

Then suddenly he was serious, and put his head on one side, considering me. He began to walk away, then turned and said:

"Once more, just one more time." And he was gone.

Damn! One more time what? One more time playing dice, one more time jumping off a cliff, one more time playing the drums. One more time what?

Only another two days to go. Great!

But it wasn't two days. The following morning a man rode up to the house on a piebald horse. I recognized him immediately as the young monk who had held the torch for us to light Anukula's pyre all those years ago. This side of the mountains he was an odd anachronism. He looked like an Indian brave complete with buckskins, but had his head shaved like all the men of his family.

He bowed formally to Connie, his face serious, then to me. It was to me he spoke.

"Mr. Gil asks that you please come now. Today. He says to tell Christie the plans you made on the mountain have been changed – he said you would know what he meant."

I tried to lever more information from him, but he remained annoyingly mute.

Connie and I threw a few things into a bag. The horses were waiting at the stables, ready saddled. I saw her hands shake on the saddle horn as she mounted – horses were not her thing and neither were mysteries.

The man set a brisk pace. Not dangerous for the terrain but fast enough for no further questions. Connie, who usually avoided horses like the plague had difficulty keeping up, so I took her reins and led her mount along the rocky path.

The cleft in the mountain rose sheer on either side, towering overhead and blocking out the sun. Then the circle of Crestone burst upon us with blinding rays of light. Connie looked around her in awe. It was like a moon crater – flat, round and surrounded by towering, snow-capped mountain peaks. Children played in the dust, school doors ajar. Adults chatted, sitting on the wall around the well. All familiar sights to me but not to Connie.

Pa had often offered to bring her, but she had always made excuses and backed out claiming fear of horses, but I think also she appreciated this was a special place for the two of us.

The holy man helped Connie from the horse while I dismounted, then motioned for us to follow.

David was standing outside the candle cabin a few hundred yards away. He was looking at us but made no move to greet us. And Pa was missing altogether. I assumed he was off walking in the mountains with one of the Lady's sons, as he often did.

He'd get a mouthful from me when he turned up. He'd put us in enough of a panic to bring us up here two days early. And Connie, who hated horses, had probably suffered the worst hours of her life.

The cabin usually rustically pretty, was especially lovely today. As we neared, we could hear the tinkle of the wind-chimes and see the candles burning within. Someone had placed garlands of mountain flowers around the door and along the edge of the roof.

Then I was glad Pa had asked me to bring Connie. She loved festivals – especially where singing and dancing were involved. We'd visited her relatives in Hawaii on a few occasions and watched the hula girls dance to native drums. She even dragged Pa up to dance once or twice which was hysterical. He was good at rhythm, but dance steps eluded him. The two of them always ended up laughing so much they'd to stop. I smiled at the memories.

Our guide had disappeared round the cabin's side and since Davy wasn't running to greet me, I ran to him. I stopped yards away. What on earth could be wrong with him?

This was David who was tough as nails. David, who's sarcastic humor could reduce a party to tears of laughter. David who loved us all, especially Pa, and always had.

I hardly knew this stranger before me.

His face was haggard and drawn and he looked on the verge of collapse. He was holding it together but only just.

At that moment, the Lady came out of her nearby home, smiling at Connie, who was still some yards behind, and inviting her to take tea. Connie looked at me and I pasted on a smile and nodded.

"Go. I'll be along in a few minutes. Get to know them – you'll love them. Go easy on the tea though. It has an unfortunate effect on me."

She laughed and the Lady took her arm, glancing anxiously back at me over her shoulder.

The smile slipped from my face as I turned back to David.

"Where's Pa?" I said, desperate not to know the answer.

Davy led me to the cabin door. Even though it was bright with candles, it took a moment for my eyes to adjust from the brilliance outside.

At first, I saw nothing, then a truckle half tucked away behind a stand of candles and covered with a blue handwoven blanket.

Davy nodded and I walked over and knelt down. My Pa was there, his eyes bright and intelligent as ever. He tried to smile but it was difficult because one side of his face drooped down, pulling the corner of his eye with it.

I didn't need to ask questions. I'd seen this before with Grace. She had temporarily recovered but I knew there was no way back for Pa.

I turned away but he put out his good right arm and gripped me hard pulling me back. He couldn't speak but we had never needed words. My Pa was devastated to be leaving us, but glad for the rest. He was in a place of peace, surrounded by votive candles which had given him comfort his entire life.

His hand was surprisingly strong, and he dragged me down to him. I rubbed my cheek against his face, but he was beyond speech.

"Shall I fetch Connie?" I whispered and he blinked his eyes in response. Davy was already out of the door.

I gripped his hand and kissed it. A tear slid from the corner of his good eye and I wiped it away.

He had closed his eyes and gone very quiet. I thought Connie was too late, but as her silhouette appeared in the doorway and cast a shadow across his pallet, he roused again and the look of love which crossed his face broke my heart.

He had planned it that she would be the last being on earth he would kiss, the last to whom he would show love. He got his wish. While her lips were pressed to his, his chest rose and fell one last time and that gentle soul with the voice of an angel was gone.

I was the one left comforting David. I'd thought I'd have been completely overcome, but perhaps it hadn't sunk in yet. I dreaded when it did.

Davy reached into his pocket and pulled out two envelopes.

"Don't ask me how the fuck he knew but he left these for you." I snatched them away from him in case Connie saw. I wanted to know what was in mine first.

I walked behind the cabin, sat on the ground and read.

At the top of the page was a little drawing of the pendant he wore always, and the message read:

"I know there is no need of words between us my darling daughter, so you'll understand this note is for my sake more than your own.

I promised you nothing would ever come between us, and you need to understand that no matter how it must appear, it won't. Not even death can take you away from me.

Anukula's lady will tell you what I want you to do.

If you are able, I would like you and Connie to fulfil my request. If it's too much to ask, I'll understand.

As I write, the music has already begun. Oh, my Christie, it is beautiful beyond words. Although it's more blues than rock and roll – sadly."

I sobbed out loud then wiped my eyes and laughed. Typical Pa – music to the end.

"Please thank my friends for their loyalty over the years. There have been times they have been with me when there was no-one else."

He'd signed it

To the only being on earth who understood the need for my spirit to soar.

With grateful love forever.

Pa

I slid sideways onto the earth and sobbed. But then my sensible side reasserted itself. I blew my nose, put my precious letter back in its envelope and returned to the candle-lit cabin.

Connie sat quietly by his side holding his hand. She had straightened the blanket and pulled it to his chin as a mother would with a child. Her eyes were dry but her expression far away. She smiled at me.

I left her alone with him and went to see the Lady. She regarded me with sympathy and offered me a cup of tea. I thought, incongruously, of the gatherings on Grace's lawn at Windham.

I asked for a glass of water. She fetched it, icy from the well, then left me alone for a while.

I don't know how much time passed, but then Connie was sitting beside me and taking my hand.

I gave her the letter Pa had left for her. She perused it briefly then folded it and put it in her pocket. She never did share it with me, and I never asked.

"Pa said you would know what this means. He wants the same farewell as Anukula. He wants the Lady and her family to make the preparations, but you and I to carry out the final act this side of the curtain."

I was horrified. The heartless bastard. How could he do this to Connie?

She squeezed my hand and said determinedly

"I don't care what it is. I will do it."

We kept vigil through the night, my mother and I. The following morning the Lady and her family had prepared the pyre and Pa's body was placed upon it with reverence. Flowers were strewn over him and over our heads as we knelt on the ground at his feet. Columbines.

Her son stood to one side with the lighted torch, and as we rose, he walked over to us.

I remembered how I had admonished Pa for his display of grief at Anukula's rites and determined to take my own advice for Connie's sake.

But she didn't need it – she was almost serene. She stood over the pyre and kissed her Gil gently on the lips, then reached to the boy for the torch.

As if she had done it a thousand times before, she thrust the flame into the pyre until one side was well and truly alight. Then she wrapped my fingers around the torch – just as I had with Pa - and lead me to do the same on the other side.

I am ashamed to say I wept uncontrollably, and my mother comforted me.

As the smoke twisted skyward and the sweet smell of rose incense filled the air, the most stunning smile lit her face.

I followed her eyes to what I always knew would be. There stood Pa – I'd say large as life if that wasn't inappropriate – punching the air like he had when he'd hit that rare top note. She was laughing and everyone around her who clearly didn't know our crazy family, was looking at her as if she'd lost her mind.

But even she didn't see what I saw. Pa carried my Trina, who looked at me shyly, her head snuggled into his chest, then he turned to me and smiled that special smile. I'd take odds on no-one seeing Jamie either – he was my special cross to bear - who grinned and stuck his tongue out at me. I reciprocated. Now they knew it wasn't only crazy Connie but completely crazy Christie as well.

My Pa had promised he would never leave us. He had never lied to me. Connie and I cried together and separately many times. Why wouldn't we? We missed him terribly. But we never grieved. He'd be back for us. Probably toting that son-of-a-bitch Jamie with him.

My Jamie grew up into a gorgeous, gentle man. He hated surfing, thankfully, but joined a band where he played guitar. He was continually compared to his famous grandfather but, I'm very pleased to say, he felt complimented rather than resentful. And why not? There would never be another Gil Robson – he was unique but then so was James Robert

Anderson as the world discovered.

Jamie reopened Pa's theater, refurbished it and named it the Gil Robson Memorial Theater. There were many shows held there but, every year on July 16th, my son would deck the stage with mountain flowers and he and his band played to Pa's friends who eventually became their own.

I was fortunate in my daughter-in-law. She was a beautiful girl with rose gold curls which reminded me of DeeDee from my Champaign days. She was kind and funny and gave me two wonderful grandchildren to brighten my days.

In times of stress, I often felt Pa's hand on my shoulder and once, after Rob died, he whispered in my ear "Be patient, my Christie."

"Easy for you to say," I grumbled under my breath.

Clearly and joyfully, I heard him laugh.

And in the end the love you take
Is equal to the love you make

Thank you for reading '**The Ultimate Link' Series**. I hope you came to care for Gil and Christie, Giulia and Connie and all their companions, loved and otherwise.

Also available from me on Amazon in paperback, hardback and Kindle:

The Life and Times of Grace Harper Maxwell

Which is the back-story to the lovely and enigmatic Grace Maxwell you've come to love in the Ultimate Link. She gives very little away so needed her own book to explain why she behaved as she did.

Your interest is greatly appreciated.

With best wishes,

Printed in Great Britain
by Amazon